I0655000

Chicago Dental Society

Proceedings of the Chicago Dental Society

at the twenty-fifth anniversary, held at the Grand Pacific hotel & the Chicago

college of dental surgery

Chicago Dental Society

Proceedings of the Chicago Dental Society
at the twenty-fifth anniversary, held at the Grand Pacific hotel & the Chicago college of dental surgery

ISBN/EAN: 9783337223205

Printed in Europe, USA, Canada, Australia, Japan

Cover: Foto ©Andreas Hilbeck / pixelio.de

More available books at **www.hansebooks.com**

PROCEEDINGS

OF THE

CHICAGO DENTAL SOCIETY

AT THE

TWENTY-FIFTH ANNIVERSARY

HELD AT

THE GRAND PACIFIC HOTEL

AND

THE CHICAGO COLLEGE OF DENTAL SURGERY,

February 5, 6 and 7, 1889.

ORGANIZED FEBRUARY 8, 1864.

CHICAGO:
THE DENTAL REVIEW COMPANY.
1889.

PRESIDENTS.

Organization...E. W. HADLEY.

1864...E. W. HADLEY.

1865...GEO. H. CUSHING.

1866...J. W. ELLIS.

1867...S. B. NOBLE.

1868...M. S. DEAN.

1869...J. H. YOUNG.

1870...GEO. H. CUSHING.

1871...GEO. H. CUSHING.

1872...J. N. CROUSE.

1873...M. S. DEAN.

1874...E. D. SWAIN.

1875...C. R. E. KOCH.

1876...D. B. FREEMAN.

1877...GEO. H. CUSHING.

1878...E. NOYES.

1879...A. W. FREEMAN.

1880...GEO. H. CUSHING.

1881...T. W. BROPHY.

1882...E. S. TALBOT.

1883...C. P. PRUYN.

1884...A. W. HARLAN.

1885...C. F. MATTESON.

1886...FRANK H. GARDINER.

1887...J. G. REID.

1888...JAS. A. SWASEY.

INDEX.

A

B

C

D

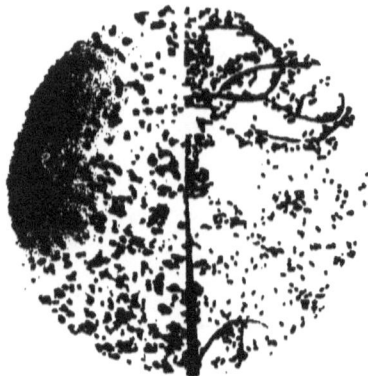

FIG. 1.
Micro-organisms found in deep seated caries. Micro- and diplo-cocci. From Dr. Miller's pure cultures.

FIG. 2.
Longitudinal and cross section of healthy, non-infected dentine. Dr. Andrews' preparation.

FIG. 3.
Longitudinal and cross section of naturally infected, carious dentine. Dr. Miller's preparation.

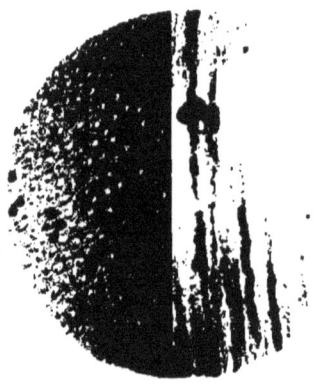

FIG. 4.
Longitudinal and cross section of artificially infected, carious dentine. Dr. Miller's preparation

FIG. 5.
Section of a cavity formed by micro-organisms. Natural decay. A, mass of micro-organisms. B, cavity formed. Dr. Miller's preparation.

FIG. 6.
(Diagramatic.) Showing the white zone of decalcified dentine at B. Micro-organisms at A. Dr. Andrews' preparation.

THE PROCEEDINGS

OF THE

CHICAGO DENTAL SOCIETY

AT THE

TWENTY-FIFTH ANNIVERSARY.

The twenty-fifth anniversary of this Society was celebrated by a three days' meeting devoted to the reading of papers and discussions on professional subjects. The sessions were held in the ladies' ordinary of the Grand Pacific Hotel, February 5, 6 and 7, 1889.

The Society was called to order by the President, Dr. J. A. Swasey, at 10 o'clock, after which the Rev. G. C. Lorimer, D. D., invoked divine blessing.

The President then made a short, neat, impromptu address of welcome.

Dr. A. H. Thompson of Topeka, Kan., read a paper as follows:

GUM-COLORED PORCELAIN FILLINGS.

I feel that I should preface my paper by reminding you in advance that the entire art of porcelain filling is yet in its most crude state, notwithstanding the fact that it has been occasionally employed by a few operators for many years.

I wish also to say that the specimens shown are very crude, having been prepared hastily for mere illustration, and some of them are my earliest experiments.

The dried and whitened teeth are also unsatisfactory for illustrating the work, and you will need to moisten the settings with the finger in order to bring out the color.

The theory of porcelain settings or inlays, for filling cavities on the anterior, visible surfaces of the teeth, has been again revived and has attracted considerable attention. There is no doubt but that porcelain possesses the most favorable qualities for imitating the natural enamel in colors and texture, of any material with which we are acquainted. We constantly employ it in the imitation of the natural teeth with the greatest success and the most complete deception in restoring whole crowns, and it really seems that we should be able to use it with equal success in the restoration of parts of crowns. This is singularly difficult, however, although the difficulties that lie in the way of its extensive application are mainly those of manipulation, for it is very refractory as a filling material. The greatest difficulty to be overcome is to make a joint with the enamel that will not be easily noticed ; but this must be accomplished before we can employ the material successfully as an invisible filling.

Porcelain setting or inlay in human enamel is closely related to the arts known as inlaying and mosaic. Inlaying is the art of filling up incised designs with a material different from the base or matrix, whether metal, wood or stone, and then finishing off and polishing all together. Mosaic is the fitting together of many pieces of colored marble, enamel, glass, etc., to form a pattern and by grinding off the ends of the rods, a picture in imperishable colors is displayed. A combination of the two is called inlaid-mosaic. There is a variety of inlaid-mosaic in ivory which consists of jewels set in ivory, of which some very ancient examples have come down to us. Our porcelain dental inlay-work is most closely related to the ivory inlay-mosaic art, the technique of which we will need to study in order to accomplish the highest degree of skill in this peculiarly artistic work. Cloisonné work is made by leaving a partition or cloison of the basis material between the inlays, such as the old ivory cloisonné mosaics or the network metal pieces. In the latter, the porcelain or enamel is baked in the cells of metal in a pattern, and the whole polished off together, leaving the metal exposed in the lines of the design. Such an effect is produced by setting a piece of porcelain with gold in a tooth, as it is separated from the basis of the enamel by a cloison of gold.

At this time it is desired to call attention to but one branch of the porcelain inlay system which has been of peculiar satisfaction to the writer and to unfortunate persons requiring such operations. It is that of filling cavities on the exposed surfaces of the necks and roots of the anterior teeth above the enamel, in the region usually covered by the gum, by setting in inlays of red or gum-colored porcelain taken from porcelain gum teeth. Gold fillings on the

necks and roots of teeth are very unsightly and offensive, and anything that will enable us to avoid such a misfortune to our sensitive patients will be a boon indeed. It is especially serious with
ladies, some of whom by too vigorous cross brushing have caused
the gums to recede over the necks of the anterior teeth, thereby
leading to caries in that location. Of course the number of cases
in which this art is applicable, are comparatively few—scarcely
enough, in fact, to develope a passable skill. But with careful
effort, the operation can be performed very nicely by the ordinary
practitioner, and the pleasure of seeing the appearance of gum
restored where an ugly carious spot or a gold filling existed before,
is a reward for the tedious labor expended in its execution. It is
the highest art to thus restore a lost part in a conspicuous place
in such a manner that the restoration cannot be detected by ordinary observation.

The technique of this branch of the work as developed by the
writer's limited practice, is very simple. A piece of porcelain
gum from an artificial tooth is selected, that matches the natural
gum in color and texture as closely as possible, there being some
variety in the color of the gum in different persons. But, as the
cement used in setting the piece is colored also, you can control
the shade to a great extent by the amount of color employed. To
color the cement, a very little dry Chinese vermilion, tinged with
ultramarine blue, is first mixed with the oxide powder to make the
cement blueish, for setting the piece, as the pink cement furnished
us will not answer for this purpose.

The piece of porcelain gum selected is ground to proper thin-
ness from the tooth-body side, making allowance for the projection
of the piece from the cavity to some extent, in order to restore the
fullness of the gum. The cavity must be cut as deeply as safety
will permit and laterally to the gum margin, or under the gum if
possible, in order to make a good joint. Large cavities running up
on the root, unless quite narrow, will require two pieces to fill properly, which are fitted together at an angle in the center, like the •
comb of a roof. The margins of the cavity must be undercut and
the thin edges of the pieces slipped into the undercuts. This
should always be done when two pieces are used. When there is
a mere crescent of decay at the margin of the enamel, the piece
requires delicate fitting, and if the crescent is very extended the
cavity can best be filled with two pieces. Large cavities including

portions of both crown enamel and neck can be filled with a combination piece of artificial tooth including crown and gum.

The inlays are very carefully ground, being fitted in the cavity
from time to time and being examined with a magnifying glass.
Care must be taken to preserve the contour of the tooth, or the
margins and long ends of the piece will not lie closely. When the
piece becomes too small or too delicate to hold in the fingers, it can
be set in shellac on the end of a piece of soft wood, and ground
safely. The shellac is easily softened in the lamp flame to change
the position of the piece, or to try it in the cavity. For very large
cavities it is sometimes best, in order to save time, to take an
impression of the cavity and have the piece roughly fitted to a
model in the laboratory.

When the piece is properly fitted in the cavity, it is set in the
colored cement, and after this has hardened the whole is carefully
ground. The inlay is allowed to project in a rounded eminence
from the cavity, in order to, in a measure, restore the contour of the
gum. The effect of this simple operation is surprising,—the deception being complete, for the artificial gum piece seems continuous
with the natural gum when moistened, and the great advantage
over gold, from an artistic standpoint, is at once apparent.

In conclusion, the writer does not wish to be considered an
expert in this work, for he is not a porcelain worker, and only
skilled porcelain workers could be expert. But the simple methods
here described and which will be demonstrated in clinic, are those
which the ordinary practitioner can employ with success with the
appliances and materials he has ready to his hand.

The porcelain inlay filling system is, of course, in its earliest
infancy; but it has a great future before it if its possibilities are
properly developed, for we can not but believe that the porcelain
filling is the filling of the future.

DISCUSSION.

Dr. C. Thomas of Iowa, in opening the discussion, said: I
hardly know how to commence my remarks on the paper which has
just been read. Dr. Thompson's process is different from the one
I use. In my process of inserting these fillings, it makes no difference what shape the cavity has so that it is retentive. Where
Dr. Thompson grinds his porcelain to fit, I make a matrix by burn-
ishing a thin piece of platinum into the cavity, making my

filling in that matrix. I then remove the platinum, and the filling is as near perfect as is necessary. I have only been using this method a short time. I had occasion, however, the other day to see several fillings that have been in two years, they were as perfect as the day they were put in. When I first commenced using gum-colored porcelain fillings a great many of my friends said to me, they will not last; they will wash out. So far I have not found any but what remain perfect. I go farther than Dr. Thompson does. He merely puts his fillings into the visible surfaces of the anterior teeth, I insert them in all cavities.

Dr. W. H. Dorrance of Ann Arbor : I rise, not because I am better acquainted with the subject than any one else, but I have a word or two to add to those of the essayist. I believe on account of the superior density of the porcelain which is taken from the artificial tooth, that it is more valuable for the restoration of corners, or that portion of the tooth which takes on considerable wear or strain in the act of mastication. While it requires a greater degree of skill and more careful manipulation to adjust pieces taken from the broken section, yet I think the results are much better than where the porcelain is baked in the' matrix of platinum. I believe porcelain fillings are valuable for certain purposes, that they are more artistic in their look and adjustment ; they will do more excellent service on account of the non-conduction of the material than any metal or gold-filling substance ; but I do not believe that the system is universally applicable — at least, this is my impression at present. I do think, however, that it is well worth the thought and effort of any practitioner, and more especially those who have not attempted it. You certainly can give yourselves much better satisfaction as well as your patients, by adopting the methods now in vogue of porcelain filling.

Dr. J. G. Reid of Chicago : I would like to ask those who have been interested in this kind of work how they would retain a porcelian filling used in the restoration of the contour of a central incisor.

Dr. Thomas : After preparing the cavity as for a gold filling, cut two retaining points. After having formed the platinum to fit the cavity, insert a platinum pin (a double-headed one) ; cut the head off, letting it extend into the porcelain. Bake the porcelain around this pin. Pay no attention whatever to contour ; the porcelain is cemented in the cavity. After the cement has thoroughly

.

hardened grind the porcelain to just the shape required, which is very easily done, and the fillings are very hard to detect. You may stand three feet from a person and not detect one. I find that in putting in these fillings, it is difficult to get the exact shade of the tooth, but I prefer having them a little darker rather than whiter.

Dr. L. L. Davis of Chicago: I have had opportunities to see quite a number of porcelain fillings inserted by Dr. Land of Detroit, which I understand is the method employed by the gentleman who opened the discussion. If the fillings I saw were a fair representation of the work that can be accomplished by this method, I would not wish to use the method in my practice. I saw a case presented before the Michigan State Society last year, for which was claimed the best results. All the anterior teeth of the patient were in an eroded condition and the enamel had been replaced by means of porcelain. The difference in the shade of the porcelain to that of the natural teeth was very apparent. There were no two patches that matched in shade. The line between the porcelain patch and the tooth looked as though a dirty thread had been tied around each tooth and the effect of the whole was, to me, disgusting.

Dr. Abbott of Iowa: I rise for the purpose of asking a question of the reader of the paper—how he manipulates the pieces he puts in to retain them?

The essayist: In my work I make two pieces of one piece, dovetailed all around; you can do this with one end or one end and a side, fitting it closely, getting as much depth as possible to the piece. The cement will hold it secure so that you can not get it out of its hold. It is not essential that it should be dovetailed if the cavity is sufficiently deep; if the cavity is shallow, however, it would be more difficult.

The idea has been advanced that cement is not effective. I have gum pieces that have been in for two years, and there is little or no effect upon the cement, and it must be borne in mind that the cement is right at the margin of the gum where the mucus would have probably more effect on it than the saliva itself, because the grooves between the piece and teeth are so small that it would take a long time to affect it.

Another point is the durability or effectiveness of the cement in excluding external moisture much more perfectly than any other filling which we use.

Dr. E. M. S. Fernandez of Chicago: This method gives us a great field for work.   My experience in porcelain fillings has been confined to crown cavities.   I have used the little tips made in England.   They are made of clear porcelain, similar to the tooth structure itself.   I shellac them on a small piece of wood, and shape to suit the case.   I prepare the cavity with corundum points.   After that is done I cement them in place with oxyphosphate.   I then take corundum wheels, and grind them down even with the surface of the tooth.   I find them useful and lasting.

Dr. C. N. Johnson of Chicago: When we have prepared a cavity with a round disc or corundum points, we find that that cavity is not perfectly done, a fissure runs from it in one or two directions, which need to be cut out.

Dr. W. X. Sudduth of Philadelphia: If you take a porcelain tip that is closely adapted to the shape of the cavity, and then put emery into the cavity, and fasten the tip to the end of an engine point, you get the same result, grinding the porcelain filling into the tooth, making a close joint.

OBTUNDENTS OF SENSITIVE DENTINE.

BY T. E. WEEKS, D. D. S., MINNEAPOLIS, MINN.

As a preface I deem it proper to briefly consider the structure and envirorment of teeth.   In this we will be aided by reference to the chart.*   The enamel, E, we know as the hardest tissue of the body; its substance is principally inorganic, containing as it does less than 4 per cent of organic matter.   Like a coat of mail, it protects that portion of the tooth above the gum from injury.   In this connection we should note that it is a poor conductor of heat and cold.   The major portion of the tooth, D, is the dentine.   It is a delicately organized structure and contains about 28 per cent of organic matter.   The microscope shows innumerable canals or tubuli, whose general direction is at right angles with the surface of the pulp; within these tubules are the dentinal fibrils, which we believe to be processes of the odontoblasts, which are the outer layer of cells of the pulp, P.   This is the tooth-builder, or formative organ.   It is made up of cells of the connective tissue group, nerves and blood vessels.   In its structure, C, the cementum or root covering, very nearly resembles bone.   By means of this

* The diagram used was an enlarged copy of Fig. 369, Vol. I, page 657, of the American System of Dentistry.—ED.

tissue the intimate connection between the highly vascular pericementum and the dense substance of dentine is made possible. P. m. indicates the pericementum or peridental membrane, which envelopes the root, acts as a cushion, and supplies vitality to the cementum. The connection between these two tissues is sufficient to insure the retention and usefulness of the tooth after the destruction of the pulp.

A, is the alveolus or bony socket of the tooth. All these parts are so closely related and interdependent upon each other as to occasion much discussion as to structure, function, etc., but experience has shown us that the portion which can be spared is the pulp, yet this should be removed only as a last resort.

The chief physical function of the pulp is the formation of dentine; after the completion of this process this function is devoted to the maintenance of vitality and the formation of protective dentine, but it has another function—the sensory—which, according to Prof. Black (American System of Dentistry, Vol. 1), is limited to "a peculiar resentment to thermal changes"— "normally a sense of pain upon sudden changes of temperature is the only *sensation conveyed to the sensorium from this organ;*" also, *degrees* of temperature can not be distinguished "unaided by the nerves of other parts, as the lips, gums and peridental membrane." This organ has not the tactile sense, and in common with all organs destitute of this sense, is capable of transmitting (when injured or irritated from whatever cause) only one sensation—pain.

The views held by Profs. Black, Stowell and others, seem to be the only logical explanation of the normal sensitiveness of dentine, viz.: that impressions are communicated to the pulp through the dentinal fibrils or processes of the odontoblasts; that anything that irritates or disturbs the distal ends of the fibrils is felt in the cells themselves, and that from the intimate relation of the odontoblasts with the nerves of the pulp, any disturbance in these cells is immediately felt by the nerve endings and thence transmitted to the sensorium, continued irritation causing increased sensory function. It might be asked how a simple protoplasmic material, such as an odontoblast, can transmit sensations, but physiology teaches that protoplasm is sensitive; that the amoeba,' leucocyte and young connective tissue cells exhibit their sensitive properties by certain *motions* when subjected to heat, cold and chemical agents. These odontoblasts and their processes being cells similar to· those experimented upon, would naturally respond in like manner to the same influences.

It is further gathered that sensation may be transmitted along the fibrils from the periphery of the dentine to the nerve endings in the pulp, in a manner similar to that manifested in the delivery of the impulse to contraction from the nerve endings along the fibrils of the striped muscles.

To quote again (American System of Dentistry, Vol. 1), "there is but one motor nerve ending in conjunction with a single muscular fibril, no matter what its length (Krause, Koelliker); this is sufficient to communicate the impulse to contraction to the whole fibre, though it may be much longer than the dentinal fibril. Here it will be seen that the passage of an impulse along a protoplasmic body *from* a nerve ending seems demonstrated. In the explanation offered of the sensitiveness of dentine, the impulse passes along a protoplasmic body *to* a nerve ending. The conduction in the two instances is the same, but the impulse travels in the opposite direction."

In a normal condition all dentine contains a certain amount of water. When this is removed the normal function of transmitting impressions seems to be suspended, or at least modified.

Various theories are advanced to explain this; that the tubuli contain only a fluid which is capable of transmitting sensation and pressure, and that this may be removed, thus destroying the function, I can not believe. But that water is present, not only as a constituent of the fibril, but also surrounding it, seems to be true; then if this fibril, being a protoplasmic mass responding to irritation by motion, may not the removal of the water surrounding it, relieve in a degree its natural restriction within unyielding walls thus allowing motion in the fibril, not restricting it to the cell itself? But is this dehydration accomplished without one of two factors; a raising of temperature by heat in the form of hot air, or lowering of temperature produced by evaporation? If the ground I have taken is tenable, either combination would produce the results desired, because it has been shown that the motions of the class under consideration are retarded and finally stopped by cold, but rendered more active by heat, which, when sufficiently increased "causes them to take on a state of tetanic contraction," thus stopping all motion.

We know that heat or cold will produce irritation or pain, also that violent or continued irritation will induce hyperæmia and inflammation ; this knowledge should cause us to proceed with extreme caution when resorting to desiccation.

Many chemical agents lower the temperature by evaporation ; some dehydrate by means of their affinity for water, as absolute alcohol. Ether and chloroform act mainly by evaporation ; others, like chloride of zinc, combine with the dehydrant action a destruc-. tion of a portion of the fibrillæ. Others again act only as anodynes; these fail wholly or in part, either because they do not act upon protoplasm at all, or becase they cannot penetrate the dense structure far enough to make their influence felt. Cocaine, while it acts readily upon the nerve endings of mucuous tissue, is inert when applied to dentine, except in certain cases of loose structure. Until recently all efforts at obtunding have been confined to the dentine, but now some efforts are being made where the result seems to be the anæsthesia of the pulp. Dr.Custer thinks that by the Ottolengui method, the pulp shares in the anæsthesia of the fibrillæ ; however he does not seem to have proven his hypothesis by the removal of a pulp after employing the method. I have demonstrated to my entire satisfaction that the application of cocaine and alcohol by electrolysis — a la Dr. McGraw—does anæsthetize the pulp, as I have removed ten pulps, all with little pain, and some with absolutely none. In the use of this method it seems that desiccation plays no part, as in all of my successful cases the dentine contained the normal amount of water. Several times our attention has been called to the influence which vibration may exert over the fibrillæ, or nerves of the pulp. It is certain that a severe shock will for the time, benumb the sensory nerves; also, that a succession of slight shocks, no one of which may be perceptible to the senses, will produce the same result. The vibratory method of Dr. Brimmer, consists in the rapid revolution of a coarse bur in close proximity to, or light contact with, the surface to be obtunded. In the organ under consideration, I think the action is upon the pulp, through the dentine, as Dr. Brimmer reports the removal of a pulp painlessly ; possibly the nerves of the peridental membrane may contribute some part.

That dentine and its fibrils may be cut with less pain with a sharp instrument and rapid motion, is as patent as that the nerves of soft tissues are often severed without sensation by a dexterous stroke of a keen blade, while intense pain is occasioned if the same

incision is made slowly, or with a dull blade ; further, this instrument, if a bur, should be so shaped as to clear itself of chips ; for
when a bur becomes clogged it ceases to cut, but revolves with
friction ; hence heat and its resultant impression—pain.   If the
cavity is dry—not necessarily desiccated—any bur will be less
liable to clog than if the cavity be moist.   The bur should also be
a small one, for it requires less pressure, consequently less friction
to make it cut.

When we come to consider cutting the dentine, we encounter
that added sensitiveness produced in the patient's mind by the
senses of sight and of hearing.

Having admitted that nerves or protoplasmic fibrils may be
severed by the flash of a keen blade, we must admit that it can be
done in very few instances, if the *patient is aware* of the action.
No dentist who has listened to the manifestations of pain (?) by
screams, during the experiment of revolving a bur in light contact
with nonsensitive enamel on the outside of a tooth, can doubt that
this hypersensitiveness is induced wholly by the mind—but how to
control it, "there's the rub ;" control this, and the reduction of
actual sensitiveness is easy.   I guess there is nothing for it but
" mind cure;" but seriously, gentlemen, do not those practitioners
possessed of strong personal magnetism, succeed best, other things
being equal.   Gaining the confidence of the patient is everything.
Much may be accomplished in this direction by a calm self-poise,
by abstaining from abrupt motions, and by an apparent confidence
begotten of a knowledge of what to do and how to do it.   Whatever
means we may employ should be with a thorough knowledge of the
structure and function of the parts involved, also, of the action of
the agent, especially if such agent may be destructive to either the
organic or inorganic structure.   With a clear appreciation of the
fact that when irritation is continued beyond a certain point,
inflammation follows, it does not seem likely that a man will daily
take the risk of passing the border line ; yet I can but feel that
when those agents or forces which may destroy are employed, that
it is playing with fire, and for myself, I prefer after a careful selection and use of instruments, to confine myself to those agents which
only lull to sleep, feeling more confident that the object of my
attentions will be more likely to awaken to health and usefulness
than by the application of harsher means.   Again, when the advocate of a new method admits that its application induces "slight

pain," I am slow to embrace it, for pain is what I would avoid, and I *know* that without any but mechanical means and careful manipulation I can perform the operation with but "slight pain."

Dr. L. E. Custer of Dayton, Ohio, in opening the discussion, said: Before speaking of obtundents proper, I desire to refer to the imagination, its relation to the cutting of sensitive dentine, and other conditions affecting it. Time is too limited to enter into the metaphysics of the subject. It should suffice to say that a painful sensation is mental activity, a mental condition, or, in other words, a mental operation. The imagination is that faculty of the representative power of the intellect whereby there is a condition for every image formed subjectively, which, for the time being, is related, so far as painful or pleasurable sensations are concerned. Actual suffering of an imaginary or painful operation is according to the cultivation of this faculty, and the manner in which it is reproduced. In the cutting of sensitive dentine the patient is in constant fear of a thrust of an instrument into the pulp. The pain induced by the blunder (and unconsciously) causes a portion of it to be associated with the present actual pain. Or, on the other hand, he may at one time have had a tooth extracted, and, both being dental operations, it is impossible for him to dissociate the pain of that operation from the present. So, then, we have this wonderful faculty to deal with in the cutting of sensitive dentine. There is probably not one here, who, at one time or another, has not had a patient in such an imaginative state of mind that the sight of instruments or medicine would produce fainting. The imagination is affected through the sense of perception, and the senses of sight, hearing and smelling are disturbed in their relations. The strongest influence comes through the sense of sight. A display of instruments will cause patients to recoil with fear. They really imagine that the greater the supply and display of fine instruments the more pain will be produced, when the contrary, as you are well aware, is the fact. On account of this play upon the imagination, the greater part of electrical apparatus should be hidden from view as much as possible, all blood and pus cleared away. On account of our patients being more largely of the gentle sex, bric-a-brac and other articles characteristic of the home should be prominent about the office.

Next to sight comes the sense of hearing. It is a most common occurrence for people to associate with noise the sense of pain, as, for instance, the bursting of a boiler or the falling of a wall with a sudden crash, carrying pain, destruction and death before it. Even the filing or cutting in a laboratory cannot be endured by all. It will be found that a very large majority of women, accustomed to the quietude of home, undergo operations with less fortitude in our offices if surrounded by noise.

The third condition through which the imagination is easily affected would be that of smell. Iodine and creasote bring to the mind of patients painful recollections. Besides these three senses there is one more important factor, and that is the personal magnetism of the operator. His approach and dealings toward his patients should be as if he were dealing with a live and sensitive human being, and not with a cadaver or wooden effigy. He should be sympathetic and perfectly aware of how much pain such operations produce. He should be familiar with his case and know just exactly what to do. He should handle his instruments gently, and all evidences of bungling and carelessness carefully guarded against.

In regard to the use of obtundents proper—as a general thing, owing to the peculiar structure of the dentine as compared with that of soft tissues, those agents which act most efficiently and most effectually upon the soft tissues have not such a profound effect upon the dentine. There is but one exception to this, and this, reduction of temperature, which acts equally well upon both whenever function may be retarded or entirely suspended by change of structure, withdrawal of nutrition, or by reduction of temperature. Change of structure is best produced by coagulation or dehydration. Carbolic acid is most easily used, but owing to its superficial effect upon the dentinal canaliculi and their contents, its effect is not very deep or thorough and can not be relied upon as an obtundent to sensitive dentine. Dehydration has more effect on the dentinal fibril than any other tissue, owing to the structure of the dentine. It has been shown why this method of change of structure is of more effect and is more easily obtained. In the perfect performance of nerve function the dentinal fibril requires moisture or water; it acts in a two fold sense—that which constitutes the fibril itself and that which concerns the space between the fibril and the walls of the canaliculi, in the former acting as a constituent, in the latter as a condition, as the end or labyrinth of the ear. Dehydration can be obtained by adding carbonate of potassium to the alcohol. Dehydration is effective just in proportion as we are able to withdraw the moisture from the dentinal fibril and the canaliculi. For withdrawal of nutrition those agents which have this effect upon the soft tissues have not such an effect upon the dentine owing to its peculiar structure.

Reduction of temperature acts alike upon sensitive dentine and upon the soft tissues. Every organism seems to demand a proper performance of nerve function which is normal. If the temperature be reduced nerve activity is lessened and anæsthesia is produced according to the departure from abnormality. This method of producing anæsthesia of the dentinal fibril is accomplished by the use of rhigolene, or the less violent agent, sulphuric ether, in the form of a spray. If it is difficult to obtain complete coagulation or dehydration, we may use a combination of methods, or may partially coagulate the albumen and partially dehydrate. Along with both of these add reduction of temperature, which will have a better effect than by any single method. A new field is open for an agent or combination of agents to produce a combination of effects. As one of the most beneficial (single) agents for operations upon sensitive dentine, I believe chloride of zinc stands at the head. It must be used with care in certain extreme cases after excavating the mesial portion of a cavity. The fluid extract of cannabis indica may also be used to advantage. I fill my cavity with oxychloride of zinc, allow it to remain until next morning, and after that the cavity is filled without pain.

The recent method given to the profession by Dr. Ottolengui for obtunding sensitive dentine, when analyzed, will be found to work in two different ways by which the nerve fibril may be obtunded—by desiccation and reduction of temperature. Chloride of zinc, as I have said, acts by "change of structure" and dehydration; the Ottolengui method acts by "change of structure" and reduction of temperature.

Dr. William H. Atkinson of New York: Judging from what I have heard, the papers and discussions have been very instructive, and some of the younger members have literally taken the wind out of the sails of some of us old fellows who have done a good deal of hard work. They say we meet here to talk about old chestnuts, and we are repeating what has been done in years gone by.

So we do, and every time we breathe we are going through an old chestnut process, but we are getting something good with every breath we take. I was almost exhausted this morning when I arrived, but after being under the inspiration of the presence of my blessed children, the tone of the papers and discussions has elevated me somewhat from the deep depression into which I had fallen.

We have just had a presentation by Dr. Custer of the mental operations that go on during the practice of our profession. According to the definition of scientists, there is only one thing which we know is a mode of consciousness, and when they say there is physical pain we are sure that they do not know of any pain only by the uncomfortable amount of that something that is within us. We are dealing now with the questions that scientists in years gone by have been groping after, and we are as little children giving delineations and interpretations of what we see before us. We are inquiring after the truth, so that we are really now the *senatori senatorum*, or the senators of the wise men of the world, and yet we can not see that we can flatter ourselves that there is anything we have done that has brought this about ; but it is our good works, our affection and regard for each other, that we meet to exchange opinions on these subjects. Our aim is to do the best we can to alleviate the sufferings of our patients, and in doing this the best agent for obtunding the sensitive nerves should be used.

I can remember well the time when I was called a tooth carpenter and nothing but a mechanic, but thank God that day is passed. Our profession has undergone wonderful changes since then; the dentist of to-day is more respected, and he has a clientele that believe in him. How blessed a thing, then, it is for brethren to believe in each other, and in the next place never to be disappointed in the trust we have put in each other.

Dr. A. H. Thompson of Topeka, Kas.:—I would like to say a few words with reference to the therapeutics of the subject. It has been my custom to treat sensitiveness by resorting to oxyphosphate fillings for a week or two weeks. I find it is a great saving of time. I mistrust all instantaneous methods for fear of injury to the pulp. My rule is to simply fill the cavity with oxyphosphate and in a week or two it will be found to give great satisfaction.

Dr. A. W. Harlan of Chicago :—The thing that excited my admiration when Dr. Weeks' paper was read was that it was not encumbered by therapeutic methods of obtunding sensitive dentine, but dealt with principles. It seems to me from much reading and some little thought devoted to this subject that we are about to arrive at a point where empiricism will have to take a back seat and science come in and prove to us that we are able to handle the subject because we know it. I suppose that I am responsible for a good deal of the therapeutical nonsense of obtunding sensitive dentine, but it was all put forth with the best intention and in the hope that something good would come of it. At those times I believed that I had discovered a reasonable panacea for obtunding sensitive dentine, the bugbear of operative dentistry. I find now that many of the agents proposed for this purpose are only useful in certain cases, and that there is no one or two or three methods of using them which will prove universally successful.

The way in which the discussion on this subject was opened by my friend, Dr. Custer, struck me as being the proper way to approach it. I find in actual experience that if you can inspire the confidence of a patient by subduing his imagination, if you please, or play upon any of those faculties that will enable him to rely on your intent to do the least possible injury to his feeling, physical or mental, that you are on the road to obtunding and making operations painless in sensitive teeth.

To come down to the specific methods of obtunding individual teeth, I have this much to say, that I distrust any method of use of the oxychlorides, with the hope of continuing the excavation of a cavity in a few days. That is also true of oxyphosphates. If a cavity is so sensitive that I am unable to operate with facility for myself or ease to the patient, and apply oxyphosphate with the hope of continuing the excavation in a few days, I find an exaggerated sensitiveness at the expiration of a week instead of a subsidence. I have sought to explain that by the fact that there may be an excess of uncombined phosphoric acid, which itself is an irritant. If such fillings are allowed to remain for a greater length of time—two or three months, or longer—the excess of acid will have become dissipated, the teeth will have become accustomed to the thermal changes.

The method of desiccation, where practicable, and not carried too far, is useful in nearly every case. The main trouble in obtaining desiccation is that powerful coagulators are used which prevent the degree of desiccation that you seek to obtain. That, I believe, may be overcome by the substitution of the essential oils instead of such agents as chromic acid, chloride of zinc, carbolic or acid. I would repeat that in employing the desiccating method better results will be obtained by the use of the essential oils, and preferably those having anæsthetic properties, as peppermint, cajuput, and a few others.

Dr. A. E. Baldwin of Chicago : This is a subject that interests us all as dentists. We have to meet it every day in our offices. I have a method that has been successful with me, and which is very simple. It is a sharp bur, used with a very rapid motion, and a light touch.

Dr. J. Taft of Cincinnati : It is hardly proper for me to be called upon to say anything upon this subject for the reason that I did not hear the paper. I infer, however, from the discussion, that the whole subject of the treatment of sensitive dentine is open for consideration. I was much pleased indeed with the remarks made by Dr. Custer. He dealt with principles rather than with modes of accomplishing certain results, but after all both are necessary. It is important to understand principles, and when that is done a correct practice will more likely be adopted.

All cases of sensitive dentine are not alike. Every case has its peculiarities—has its individualities modified by the tissue itself—modified by the influence to which it has been subjected—modified by the constitution with which it is associated, and by the condition in which that constitution is at the time. Now, all will recognize the fact that an enfeebled patient, one who has not the usual vigor and strength, one who is not for the time being well nourished, one who is for the time being under the influence of irritation, is far more subject to this peculiar condition of dentine. Every patient that comes into the hands of the dentist should be scrutinized as to this general condition.

There are all degrees of sensitiveness from that which is just appreciable under contact or thermal change, to that which is most intense and unbearable, as patients will tell us many a time. These conditions ought not to be overlooked.

Then, again, the extent of this affection may be, as you know, merely superficial. You will find when, by a sharp-cutting instrument, a very superficial layer of dentine has been cut away, that the sensitiveness is gone. In some instances this condition pervades the entire dentine of a tooth. Examining a tooth in this condition by cutting into a fissure or the dentine, it will be found sensitive everywhere. These conditions must be noted, and their variations or peculiarities will indicate the precise method of procedure.

One point mentioned was the expectant method of treatment, using oxyphosphate filling for its reparative effect. I do not use oxyphosphates with which to accomplish this result, preferring gutta-percha because it is a non-irritant non-conductor. But this remedy is not applicable in all cases. Where the condition pervades all the dentine, other treatment, such as building up the system, giving it tone, is a necessity. We cannot derive from the local treatment in some cases the benefit desired. There is no such thing as striking upon some particular mode of treatment and management that will yield good results in all cases. Every case requires its peculiar treatment, according to the conditions that exist.

A STUDY OF THE EFFECTS OF COCAINE UPON MAN AND SOME OF THE LOWER ANIMALS.

BY C. P. PRUYN, M.D., D.D.S., CHICAGO, ILL.

Next to averting death, the highest prerogative of the medical man of to-day is the annihilation of pain. And in so far as he is able to meet this want of suffering humanity without dangerously interfering with life's nutritive forces will he merit success in the practice of his profession. The introduction of ether, chloroform and nitrous oxide marked an epoch in general surgery; and therewith a blessing was conferred upon mortal man which has been the means of saving thousands of lives where one has been lost from the effects of these agents.

Ever since the days of Wells and Morton, other active minds have been anxiously seeking for some safe means of producing local anæsthesia, and while we have not yet arrived at that point for every case, it remained for Dr. Koller of Vienna, to startle the world with the results of his experiments made with cocaine. This new remedy, about which so much has been written as a local anæsthetic, is classed along with such drugs as caffeine and theine, although there have been some cases reported in our late literature where the attempt has been made to antidote its effects with these remedies.

It is quite similar in its action in small doses to caffeine and theine. If it is analogous to caffeine and theine in its effects, they

can not be antidotes.   Caffeine and theine are recommended as
antidotes, but they are not, as they each have a similar action.   It
has been used in the form of elixirs and wines and in various other
forms medicinally, but some of our eminent physicians and neu-
rologists, who are making a study of it, report the unpleasant
effects that follow from its continued use to be so detrimental to the
general health, that I see no field at all in general medicine for
cocaine.   I see no place where other drugs can not take its place
and do better work.   The only use I find for cocaine is for the surgeon and rhinologist.   The results have proven unsatisfactory
where it has been used in general medicine, as it has led to the
cocaine habit, which has an effect much worse than the opium
habit.   There are in our asylums and hospitals at the present time
quite a number of victims to the cocaine habit, but they have become so—not all, but most of them—because they learned that cocaine was an antidote to morphine, and feeling the bondage
they were in to this opium habit, they wanted to break from it.   So
they began the use of cocaine, and while they have broken up the
morphine habit, they have contracted a worse habit.   So when you
hear physicians and others say there are many who have become
cocaine victims, make up your mind that they were first morphine
victims.   We have had one very marked case in our city: A
physician who from hard work and being up nights considerably
became so nervous that he could not sleep readily.   He took a
little morphine to produce sleep, and thus became addicted to its
use, and the desire for it grew upon him until he became thoroughly
addicted to the opium habit.   He realized his condition, saw it was
injuring him, and then began taking cocaine as an antidote until
he became a total wreck.   It destroys worse than opium, alcohol or
hasheesh, and I fully endorse the language of Dr. Mattison, when
he says:

"I think it for many—notably the large and enlarging number
of opium and alcohol habitues—the most facinating and seductive,
dangerous and destructive drug extant; and, while admitting its
great value in various disordered conditions, earnestly warn all
against its careless giving in these cases, and especially insist on
the great danger of self-injecting, a course almost certain to entail
added ill.   And the need of caution against free and frequent use
obtains in other cases, for there may come a demand for continued
taking that will not be denied."

So when you think of prescribing cocaine, or using it in dental surgery think also of the dangers into which it leads your patient.

In my experiments I have noticed in a very few cases where a small amount has been given, even as small as an eighth of a grain, one of the first effects to be hyperæsthesia. The patient shows great evidences of joy, of pleasure unbounded. After a little, as you give more of it, other symptoms are produced, but not this symptom of great joy. Loquacity is one of the marked physiological symptoms. A short time since I operated upon a lawyer, for whom I had just administerd a small dose of cocaine, a man who is generally very quiet in my office, but I wanted to see if the effect would be as I thought it might, so I sounded him upon a subject that I thought he would like to talk upon if I got him started, and away he went—could hardly stop talking. His talkativeness was followed with nasuea and peculiar muscular weakness. He tried to rouse himself and get out of this peculiar feeling, but he could not do it, and it was an hour before he was entirely relieved from the effects.

I take the liberty to quote an abstract from an article in a recent journal, where a gentleman had an experience that I should dislike very much to have. He did not know what it was, and heads his article, "Was it Cocaine?" as follows:

"A dentist being called in to extract the carious teeth, and finding the patient very nervous, gave a whisky toddy, followed by three hypodermic injections into the gum of a six per cent solution of Cocaine Mur." But the doctor does not state the number of minims or drachms of the six per cent solution that was used, so that our investigations into the history of the case as he reported it are somewhat in the dark. He states that she fainted immediately after the injections. The physician arrived in the course of fifteen or twenty minutes afterward, and found her in the following condition: "Insensible, pupils widely dilated, jaws locked, head drawn back, the extensors of the arms contracted and hands clinched, feet extended and incurved, breathing very rapid (about 40 per minute) superficial and spasmodic, pulse 80 and rather hard, surface cold."

"I had her inhale aromatic spirits of ammonia and the extremities rubbed vigorously with mustard. In a few minutes her respiration was fuller and easier, the extremities relaxed, but the trismus and insensibility remained. In ten minutes she had another convulsion in which the opisthotonos was well marked, this spasm lasting

about ten minutes altogether. The same treatment was administered as in the preceding convulsion, but apparently without result.
This convulsion had barely passed off when another came on of a
like severity and duration. After this, the third convulsion, the
trismus was less marked, and with some difficulty she swallowed a
half drachm each of F. Ex. Lobelia and Tr. Asafœtida (the only
antispasmodic at hand). She had one convulsion about twenty
minutes after this, but it was much milder than the preceding ones.
After this she was thoroughly relaxed and very prostrate, her only
complaint being of soreness throughout the muscular system, and a
sense of weakness."

My point is, no man ought to use cocaine who has not administered it to some of the lower animals, or until he has seen some
deaths from it among the lower animals. There the symptoms
become so marked that he can readily recognize them in the human
subject when even slightly shown. This man when he asks "Was
it cocaine?" states the symptoms as I have observed them in my
experiments, but, if I had not experimented, I would not have
known them so thoroughly, because I have never had a patient
get in this condition and I would have doubted whether these
symptoms were cocaine, or whether it was the result of shock,
but, having experimented upon dogs, I know at once when I see
these symptoms in the human subject what they are, and what to
do, because they are similar to symptoms I have observed in the dog."

"It appears that cocaine is capable of producing tetanic convulsions when administered in large doses; but the short space of
time that elapsed between the administration and the onset of the
convulsions would leave the question an open one. I may add also,
that the surface temperature was never raised above normal, and
that she had no inclination to sleep, for several hours after the convulsions had ceased."

Dr. J. Leonard Corning of New York, has published a book on
"Local Anæsthesia," wherein he gives his method of using cocaine
with a clinical history of a large number of interesting cases in
the use of this drug. He uses cocaine in general surgery, in a
very weak solution, and employs it for amputations, capital operations, in the removal of tumors, and the like. His method is a very
good one. He first exsanguinates the part to be operated upon by
the use of the Esmarch bandage up to the seat of the operation. Then with a fold on the opposite side of the extremity

operated upon, he passes beyond the part to be treated, and makes one or two wraps of the bandage, when a one or two per cent solution of cocaine is superficially injected. Then, with a long needle, he penetrates the deeper tissues, even to the bone, with five, ten or fifteen minims of this weak solution, when he is enabled to operate upon both the soft and hard tissues, painlessly. As soon as this last injection is made, a tourniquet is applied to the body portion of the extremity, which prevents the drug being carried into the general circulation, and in this manner the anæsthesia of the part may be made complete for several hours. Then, after the operation is completed, the tourniquet is gradually loosened, in order that the drug may be slowly carried into the general circulation, and, in this way, so diluted and dissipated that the systemic effects are almost, if not quite, nil; and why? Because he has all the effects of the drug held in just the part of the body that he wishes to operate upon. The circulation of the part having been suspended, or nearly so, the drug is held in just that position where he wishes it for hours, if he so desires. When we operate upon the mouth it is almost impossible to exsanguinate, or remove the blood, from that part of the body, so when we operate upon the mouth the effects are lost within a short time. Upon other parts of the body where it is impossible to apply the Esmarch bandage, he uses rings of various devices, also hæmostatic clamps, which, by pressure, incarcerate the cocaine in the field of the operation. If we could make use of a similar method upon the parts we operate upon, I feel satisfied that we could use this valuable drug with much less danger than attends our present use of it, for it is a fact that while a comparatively large amount may be used in the system at parts remote from the nerve centers, a very small amount injected into the vascular tissues, that we as dentists operate upon, may, and does often, cause very grave symptoms. Our operations are all near the main nerve centers that control circulation and respiration, and the drug, carried as it is by the circulation, has only a short distance to travel before it acts upon the peripheral nerves that convey sensation to these centers, and a disturbance of the nervous equilibrium is very soon manifest. Cerebral anæmia, even to the point of syncope, is sometimes seen with even a very small dose, and within three or four minutes after the drug has been injected, which is an illustration of the theory just advanced.

If we could devise a system of clamps that could be applied to different portions of the jaw, so as to hold in abeyance the blood supply, the probabilities are that we could use a larger amount of the drug, with little or no fear of toxicological effects being shown. As we operate now, without such appliances, the anæsthesia lasts, as a rule, not more than ten or fifteen minutes, as I have observed it.

When cocaine first came into use many men said, "Well, we use it, and it is a failure. We use it hypodermically, and get no anæsthesia. It does not lessen the pain of extraction with me." They say it is impossible theoretically to have a remedy that will act upon that dense, bony structure. My experience is just the opposite. I say I use it and I find it satisfactory. Another man uses it and he says it does not act as an anæsthetic. The difference is largely in the method of using it I think. Instead of injecting it into the periosteum, he injects it into the gum tissue, whereas I inject it, for operations upon the bone, for the extraction of teeth, for the removal of portions of the jaw, into the periosteum. If you inject it into the gum tissue, it acts as an anæsthetic on that part, that is all, and if the tissue is very loose and flabby, the injection is so quickly dissipated that the anæsthesia is only partial. If you want it for an anæsthetic in the extraction of teeth, you must inject it in the way just described, to produce the best results.

It requires much greater skill to give a hypodermic injection for a surgical operation upon the jaws than it does to give an ordinary hypodermic injection where there is an abundance of tissue in which to place the needle. You know how the ordinary hypodermic point is made. It is quite long, and if left in that condition you may get it caught in the bone, and then it bends, or prevents you putting it in as far as you wish to have it. My method is to take the ordinary hypodermic point, as it comes from the shops, and place it on an Arkansas stone and grind the extreme penetrating point so that it is comparatively blunt, or with only about one-half the beveled edge that it has for ordinary uses.

The syringe should have a minim gauge, a glass barrel, and finger guards, and should be kept absolutely clean, and never used for any other purpose, and before using should be made thoroughly aseptic. In making the injection, great care must be taken to inject no air into the tissues. This may be avoided by drawing the solution into the syringe, then turning the point upward, and expelling the liquid.

To avoid running the point against the edge of the alveolus, and also to avoid the thick, tough margin of the gum, let the point enter one-eighth of an inch from the margin, and following the surface of the bone, press it in at least three-eighths of an inch. If the beveled side of the point is held against the bone, it will avoid sticking into it. Press on the piston gently, so as to expel the liquid a drop at a time. In this way, the only pain caused is just as you pass through the mucous membrane, and this pain can be prevented by painting the part with the solution before you attempt the injection. Now as you inject a drop at a time it anæsthetizes the tissue just in advance of the point. After injecting, hold the instrument in position about a minute, so that the liquid may be taken up by the tissues and not spurt back when the point is removed. Unless this precaution is observed, the solution is liable to pass back into the mixed fluids of the mouth and be swallowed, which is very apt to produce severe nausea and emesis. Pursue this same method on both the labial and lingual sides of the tooth. Three drops of a four per cent solution on either side, as just described, injected well into the periosteum, will so thoroughly anæsthetize the soft and hard tissues that tooth extraction, or the complete removal of the bone may be effected painlessly in almost all cases. The pain of the injection is very slight, and if the syringe is thoroughly aseptic, no abscesses will follow, and the wound made by the point will usually heal by first intention. In taking impressions in cases where there is great irritability of the soft palate, an application to the mucous membrane of that part, of a four per cent ethereal solution is usually satisfactory.

I am often asked " Upon what tissue does it act best in the mouth?" I find from experience that it acts best upon the dense, fibrous gum tissue. Of course, you know there is a difference in different mouths. In one there may be an abundance of loose, flabby tissue, and the effects of cocaine in such cases would be less profound than where the tissue is fairly healthy, and of dense, fibrous texture, because in the dense tissue the drug is held just at the point you wish to have it, whereas in the other case, on account of the looseness of the texture, the effects are dissipated. For that reason in the extraction of wisdom teeth, particularly in the lower jaw, the results are not as satisfactory, because you cannot get into the dense, fibrous tissue, as you would like.

Its physiological action in small doses is to produce cerebral hyperæsthesia, dilatation of the pupils, loquacity, joyful intoxication, with a peculiar feeling of restfulness and peace with all mankind. The line of demarcation between the physiological and toxicological effects is so faintly drawn that it is impossible to tell where the one ends and the other begins. In some cases the poisonous effects may be shown at once, even from a very minute dose, while in other cases the various physiological stages are well marked and the poisonous symptoms not exhibited until a very large amount of the drug has been given. The usual poisonous symptoms are first shown by an increase of circulation, with an increase in the number of respirations and a decrease in the depth of the same, sometimes quite marked. Another early symptom may be syncope; or that peculiarly disagreeable feeling that precedes fainting. It is a very unpleasant feeling and may come on almost instantly. Your needle may be hardly removed from the gum tissue before the patient begins to show signs of syncope, palpitation of the heart, dyspnœa, præcordial pains, a sensation of stifling, or inability to obtain air may be experienced, dryness of the mouth and fauces, thirst, also tingling of the extremities, muscular weakness, cold sweats, peculiar muscular movements, almost amounting to convulsions, and if not interfered with will doubtless go into convulsions, a peculiar pendulous oscillation of the head and muscular inco-ordination.

Its chief action seems to be upon the nerve centers. In frogs it first paralyses the terminations of the sensitive nerves, and afterward abolishes reflex action. In the mammalia it first stimulates all the nerve centers, and especially the psycho-motor nerve centers. This general excitation is followed by a slight enfeeblement. Small doses increase reflex action. Large doses tend to paralyze. Respiration and circulation are quickened, except by fatal doses. The blood pressure is increased by the stimulation of the vaso-motor centers. Large doses naturally have an opposite action and lower the blood pressure. The inhibitory nerves of the heart are readily excited by medium doses. The striated muscles are not directly influenced by cocaine. Acute poisoning by cocaine causes muscular spasms, and, in consequence, a marked elevation of the temperature. Death appears to result from asphyxia, caused by respiratory paralysis, the heart continuing to beat after respiration ceases.

In my practice while I have some times been a little annoyed by the slight poisonous effects that have been manifest, I have never given enough of the drug to cause me to feel alarmed, but if I had not experimented on some of the lower animals, symptoms I have seen, in the human subjects, would have alarmed me.

Now, what should be the treatment? A careful watch should be kept over the patient, and any signs of heart failure or dyspnœa should be treated at once. If you have the symptoms of syncope, why treat for syncope, by everting your patient, putting his feet higher than his head, slapping the face with cold, wet towels vigorously, application to the nostrils of strong spirits of ammonia, or nitrite of amyl, or the Sylvester method of artificial respiration; injections of brandy, or alcohol, aromatic spirits of ammonia, both hypodermically, and by the mouth; injections of morphia, a quarter-grain, unless your patient is known to have an idiosyncrasy against morphia. Two or three drops of the nitrite of amyl on a handkerchief will probably be enough at a time, as this is a powerful drug, and needs to be used with great care. Do not lose sight of the beneficial effects to be derived from artificial respiration, for if this drug kills by paralysis of the respiratory centers, the simple fact of mechanically sustaining respiration may be the means of sustaining the life of the patient. Thirty drops of the aromatic spirits of ammonia given by the mouth, and repeated two or three times, or even more, if necessary. It might be wise to give this ammonia preparation a few minutes before beginning the operation as a prophylactic. An eighth grain of morphia hypodermically, a half hour before administering the cocaine, is another very wise prophylatic measure to adopt. As the systemic effects of cocaine are so very rapid, and the effects of morphia so comparatively slow, and as one drug seems to be an antidote to the other, it would seem to be theoretically correct to first give the morphia, and when its effects are apparent administer the cocaine, and not wait to give the morphia after the poisonous effects of the cocaine are shown.

While in actual practice, morphia seems to be an antidote to cocaine, the method of using it after the cocaine symptoms present, is like putting a policeman on a freight train to catch a thief who has just departed on the lightning-express.

Believing that morphia is an antidote to cocaine, I instituted a series of experiments, combining the two drugs in one solution, and where this combination was used the toxic effects of cocaine were manifested, even when a very small amount was administered, which seems to show that positive antagonism exists between these two drugs when used in the same solution.

The following clinical history of a series of experiments that I have made upon dogs may serve to point out more fully the dangers of the drug when given in large doses :

EXPERIMENT NO. I. (FEMALE ADULT DOG.)
Four Per Cent Solution Cocaine Hypodermically.

9:00 Minims 30 or grains $1\frac{1}{10}$.
9:10 Minims 30.   Labored and irregular pulse.
9:15 More irregular and weaker.
9:20 Minims 30.
9:30 Minims 30.   Heart weaker and slower.
9:40 Minims 30.
9:50 Minims 30.
10:00 Minims 30.
10:05 Minims 30.
10:10 Minims 30.
10:15 Minims 30.
10:20 Minims 30.
Total $13\frac{2}{10}$ grains.

Various stages, as follows :

At first expressions of great delight and joy, such as a favorite dog might show upon the return of his master after an absence of several days.

Pupils dilated—she gradually becomes quiet and apparently apprehensive of some approaching evil.   Head begins to move about from side to side, with an occasional sudden drop of head, as if to avert a blow on the top of the cranium; then rhythmical, pendulous oscillations of head from side to side; next begins to walk rapidly back and forth in the same line, or in a circle; next moves the body around and around in a circle, as if the hind legs were a pivot, Next muscular inco-ordination shown most markedly in the hind parts; hind quarters of the dog weave about from side to side, with final loss of control of the whole system, when tetanic spasms ensue, which gradually become more frequent and severe until death.

EXPERIMENT NO. 2.
Four Per Cent Solution Cocaine.

9:40 Minims 45.
9:45 Muscular Tremors.
9:50 Minims 30.
10:00 Minims 30.
10:10 Minims 30.
10:20 Minims 30.
6⅘ grains in all.

In this case exhilaration was first shown ; next that peculiar apprehensiveness of approaching evil ; then an uneasy nervous walk back and forth over the same ground for fifteen or twenty minutes, then the pendulous oscillations of the head, which gradually passed away with complete recovery, apparently, in a few hours.

EXPERIMENT NO. 3.

Twelve Per Cent Solution Cocaine Hypodermically,

9:15   Minims 25 or grains 3.
10:00 Minims 25.
10:15 Nausea and emesis.
10:20 Very restless and nervous.
10:35 Moving about in a circle as if the hind legs were a pivot.
11:00 Minims 25.
11:10 Quite excited and moves rapidly.
11:15 Down on his hind legs, but after a strong effort gets up again and moves about very excitedly.
11:18 Minims 25.
11:20   Severe tetanic spasm same as the one that died as narrated above.   Death expected every minute.
11:22 Gave hypodermically morphia, grains $\frac{1}{4}$ and Atropia, grains $\frac{1}{150}$. Spasms ceased *at once* and the whole condition of the dog changed almost as quick as lightning—changed from that very severe condition of muscular contraction to that of comparative calm and easy relaxation.

Respirations nearly normal in frequency and depth. Now as it was 12:00 o'clock, midnight, and the dog seemed so much easier, although somewhat restless, and inclined to walk back and forth the length of the room, we gave him as a final night-cap Morphia grains $\frac{1}{4}$, Atrophia grains, $\frac{1}{150}$.

At 8:30 the next morning he had apparently not slept at all during the night, as the same peculiar restlessness was still markedly shown and the dog still walking, keeping up an almost incessant movement of the whole body. Pupils still dilated and general symptoms of great weariness, continual whining and some nausea. Now gave Morphia grains $\frac{1}{4}$, Atropia grains $\frac{1}{150}$ — he soon slept and in three hours the only abnormal symptoms were great weariness and in three days he was apparently as well as ever.

This dog had 100 minims of a 12 per cent solution, or grains 12, and had arrived at the first part of the last stages of cocaine poisoning, viz.: the tetanic spasms, and when at that stage, when death seemed imminent in a very few minutes, Morphia $\frac{1}{4}$ with

Atrophia $\frac{1}{130}$ stopped at once the spasm and the muscular rigor that has always preceded death in all dogs I have killed by this drug, which seems to show that opium is an antidote to cocaine — at least in the case of dogs. The condition of insomnia has always characterized the effects of a toxic dose in my observation on both man and the lower animals.

EXPERIMENT NO. 4. (YOUNG ADULT DOG.)

A Twelve Per Cent Solution of Cocaine given Hypodermically.

9:15 Minims 25 or grains 3.

9:30 Very Tremulous.

9:40 Opisthotonos — Pupils Dilated.

9:50 Tail wags and the dog seems better.

10:10 Mouth open, tongue out and panting quite hard.

10:20 Spasmodic efforts to breathe.

10:25 Better and exhilarated.

10:55 Much better and feeling very sociable and pleasant.

11:00 Light spasm, but soon recovered with a little weariness shown the next day. In this case with a 3 grain dose we have the physiological effects shown and also the toxicological effects, which are more shown than I have ever seen them in the human subject or care to see.

EXPERIMENT NO. 5. (YOUNG ADULT DOG).

Twelve Per Cent Solution Cocaine Hypodermically. Pulse 116.

2:30 Injected 25 Minims, felt well; wanted to play.

2:35 Felt queer—looking as though listening. Standing still, licking chops; some dilating of pupil. Pulse 88—irregular.

2:45 Increase of these symptoms with muscular weakness.

2:55 Minims 25. Head constantly moving as though choking; trying to back away, still licking chops. Pulse full and regular—rapid.

3:05 Pulse 108. Constantly moving as though in play—emesis; increase of dyspnœa.

3:10 Same as before. Muscular movements weak and inco-ordinate. Keeps moving without making headway; turns as though on a pivot.

3:25 Minims 25.

3:35 Minims 25.

3:50 Symptoms improve for a few minutes, when severe spasms set in which result in death after ten minutes of severe struggling.

EXPERIMENT NO. 6. (YOUNG ADULT SKYE-TERRIER.)

Ten Per Cent Solution Cocaine Hypodermically.

7:25 Minims 25 or grains 2½.

Very quiet for ten minutes, then very restless and uneasy, moving about as if in a cage; walking back and forth.

8:00   Better.
8:05   Minims 13 or grains 1¼.
8:08   Very unsteady in his movements; muscular inco-ordination; most marked in the hind legs. Tetanic spasms—worse.
8:10   Morphia ¼. Atropia 1-150.
8:15   Morphia ¼. Atropia 1-150.
8:20   Died in a severe spasm.

Post mortem revealed a temperature intensely high ; the whole viscera seemed like a furnace so intense was the heat.

Lungs congested—heart, right side, engorged with very black blood.

Kidneys congested alsò.

It took only 3 ¾ grains to kill this one, and the antidotal powers of morphia in this case seems to have been nil.

EXPERIMENT NO. 7. (LARGE BLACK DOG.)

Ten Per Cent Solution Cocaine Hypodermically.

9:00   Minims 12½ or grains 1¼
9:15   Slight effects.
9:25   Minims 12½.
9:35   Minims 12½.
9:50   Minims 12½.

9:55   Slight pendulum-like motion of head. Seems to feel very queer and apprehensive of some approaching injury.

10:00   Minims 12½. Licking his chops and very uneasy.

10:25   Minims 12½.

10:40   Very restless and turns around with his hind parts as a pivot.

10:45   About to go into spasm when Morphia grains ¼ Atropia ₁₄₀ is given, when he improves at once and is apparently all right the next morning.

This Dog had 7½ grains during an hour and a half with an antidote of Morphia ¼ grains and came out of it all right, but was killed the next night with the same amount used, viz: 7½ grains with no morphia.

EXPERIMENT NO. 8. (SMALL DOG.)

Cocaine Hydro-chlorate Ten Per Cent.

9:00   Minims 12½ or 1¼ grains.

9:15   Dog appears very uneasy, and like the other experiments apparently apprehensive of some approaching physical danger. Pendulous motion of head.

9:25   Minims 12½. Movement of head increasing.

9:35   Minims 12½.

9:50 Tetanic spasms; not very severe, and soon pass off; then nausea and vomit. Severe spasms soon set in, and death results at 9:55. This dog succumbs at 55 minutes from the first introduction of the drug into his system, with only 3¾ grains. Post mortem reveals lungs congested, right heart distended and engorged with very black blood. Left heart nearly or quite empty. Kidneys also congested.

EXPERIMENT NO. 9. (LARGE DOG.)

Ten Per Cent Solution Hydro-chlorate of Cocaine.

8:05 Minims 25, or grains 2½.

8:10 Restless. Head moves from side to side. Licks his chops. Tail wags. Moves uneasily about the room. Whines.

8:25 A little better. Effects of the drug not so apparent.

8:30 Minims 12½, or grains 1¼. He now begins his tramp about the room. Very restless and uneasy.

8:45 Acts a little better.

8:55 Minims 12½, or grains 1¼. No increase of the effects of the drug are seen for five minutes.

9:00 P. M. Minims 25, or grains 2½ are given.

9:05 Moves about in a circle as though the hind parts were a pivot on which the body turns. He now begins to pant and appears to have great trouble in breathing.

9:10 Severe spasms of a tetanic nature set in and he continues from one spasm to another for the space of ten minutes, when death relieves him of his sufferings.

This dog was operated upon twenty-four hours previously and the same amount of the drug used, viz., 7½ grains, and just as he appeared to be going into one of the spasms a hypodermic of morphia, grains ¼, with atropia, grain ¹/₁₀₀ were given, which saved his life at that time.

Now in this experiment he is given the same amount of cocaine as on the previous occasion, and without the antidotal effects of morphia dies with the usual tetanic spasms.

It is not necessary to enlarge upon this clinical history, but simply to give you the benefit of my researches, which seem to show that morphine is an antidote to cocaine.

I have a record of over 500 cases where I have used this drug in actual practice. I have here that report, or rather the original case book, giving the details in full of each case with its clinical history.

The author has a tabulated record of over five hundred cases where cocaine was used in his practice, and the following thirty are taken from the Case Book just as they appear there. A four per cent aqueous solution of the hydrochlorate of cocaine was used in all these cases, hypodermically. Latterly he has been using a smaller amount, not more than one-half the amount used in the first fifty-six cases, and the anæsthesia has been quite as profound, and the toxic effects very rarely seen.

Case.	Age.	Sex.	Physical Condition.	Amount Injected.	Operation.	Amount of anesthesia.	Pulse.	Respiration.	Nervous Condition.	Remarks.
1	25	M.	Nervous anemia.	m. VIII.	Removal first molar.	Complete.	Normal.	Normal.	Normal.	
2	30	M.	Good.	In 2 injections m. v.	Removal low molar. Dead.	Partial.	Normal.	Normal.	Normal.	
3	31	F.	Good.	m. XII.	Excavating cavity in left upper bicuspid.	Complete.	Nor. or a lit. ab.	Slightly ab. normal.	Slight excitement.	
4	31	F.	Good.	m. II.	Wedge bet. low. cusp., and excavation of cavity.	Complete.	Normal.	Normal.	Normal.	
5	31	F.	Good.	m. VI.	Ext. three roots of upper molar.	Complete.	Normal.	Normal.	Normal.	Nausea and retching; no food had been taken for 36 h.; ext. of upper teeth very satisfactory.
6	29	F.	Good.	m. X.	Ext. first molar and second bicus. left upper.	Complete.	60	Below normal.	Slight excitement.	Lower unsatisfactory.
7	29	F.	Good.	m. VI.	Lower wisdom.	Not at all.	Normal.	Normal.	Normal.	Pain was somewhat mitigated.
8	22	F.	Good.	m. V.	Prep. of cavity of R. L. 1st molar buccal surface.	Partial.				
9	37	F.	Good.	m. VIII.	Opening through alveolus for abscess 1st R. L. bicuspid	Complete.	Lively.	Little above normal.	Normal.	Patient satisfied that the pain was mitigated.
10	19	F.	Good.	m. VI.	Prep. of cavity R. L. cuspid	Partial.	Normal.	Normal.	Normal.	
11	48	M.	Good.	m. XV.	Ext. R. L. second molar.	Complete.	Normal.	Normal.	Normal.	
12	48	M.	Good.	m. IV.	Ext. R. U. cusp. Undeveloped very long and difficult.	Complete.	Normal.	Normal.	Normal.	Suffered a little pain at the last —long operation.
13	24	F.	Good.	m. X.	Ext. L. L. 1st bicuspid. Removal of large mole on chin.	Complete.	Normal.	Normal.	Normal.	
14	13	M.	Good.	m. VIII.	Ext. R. U. first molar.	Nearly complete.	Normal.	Normal.	Normal.	Slight depression following.
15	29	F.	Slight fig.; frail; small; Frail; suff'd fr'm nerv. prostrat'n for 2 years	m. XII.	Ext. right low, third molar.	Nearly complete.	120	30	Hysteria at times, but not bad.	Dyspnœa, garrulous, muscular weariness for several hours, and sick several days following. The same am't given one week later for a like operation on opposite
16	22	F.		m. V.	Wedge between first and second molars.	Nearly complete.	150	40		side mouth, with anæsthesia complete; no systemic observ'le.
17	20	F.	Good.	m. XII.	Ext. r. L. second molar.	Partial.	Normal	Normal.	Normal.	Dyspnœa; musc'r weakn's; hyst'l.
18	48	M.	Syphilitic.	m. XII.	Ext. l. L. 1st molar and cutting away carious bone.	Complete.	N.	N.	N.	Patient says was some mitigat'n of pain; partial success only.

No.	Sex	Condition	Amount	Operation	Anæsthesia				Remarks
19	M.	Syphilitic.	m. XII.	Cutting away carious bone outer plate of alveolus over L. U. central.	Nearly complete.	N.	Normal.	Normal.	Peculiar feeling for several hours after; nervous; a little dizzy.
20	F.	Good.	m. v.	Excavating cavity in R. L. 1st molar buccal surface.	Partial.	N.	Normal.	Apparently normal at time of operation. Normal.	
21	M.	Good.	m. v.	Removing sequestrum of bone from outer plate alveolus.	Complete.	N.	Normal.	Normal.	Patient very susceptible to pain before using; very quiet after; no pain when fitting the band; patient pleased.
22	F.	Good.	m. X.	Fitting band for G. crown.	Complete.	N.	Normal.	Normal.	
23	F.	Good.	m. v.	Prep. of very sensitive cavity.	Complete.	N.	Normal.	Normal.	
24	M.	Good.	m. v.	Wedged bet. upper centrals and excavating cavity.	Nearly complete.	N.	Normal.	Normal.	
25	M.	Anæmic overworked nervous.	m. XII.	Ext. R. L. third molar.	Complete.	N.	Normal.	A very little excitement. Normal.	
26	M.	Anæmic overworked nervous.	m. X.	Ext. L. U. third molr. Ext. R. L. 2nd bicuspid.	Complete.	N.	Normal.	A very little excitem't; talkative.	Experienced some pain.
27	M.	Frail, Dyspeptic.	m. XX.	Ext. R. L. 2nd molar and roots of 1st molar.	Nearly complete.	Above Normal.	Strictly above normal.	Tremulous.	
28	F.	Good.	m. X for each tooth.	Ext. both U. third molar.	Complete.	Normal.	Normal.	Good.	
29	M.	Good.	m. XII.	Ext. L. L. 2nd molar.	Complete.	A little above N.	A little above normal.	Tremulous.	
30	F.	Good.	m. XII.	Ext. R. U. 1st bicus.	Complete.	Normal.	Normal.	Normal.	

DISCUSSION.

Dr. Templeton of Pittsburg: Have you noticed any toxic symptoms in the use of the drug?

The Essayist : Yes, sir. I have used it in almost all kinds of cases, and I cited instances where I would refrain from using it. I recall one case in which only a four per cent solution was used, and the toxic effects were quite marked, there being hysteria, etc. In such cases I would avoid its use. Some people have heard of co-caine, and are greatly alarmed the very moment you mention it to them. The thought or fear, acting upon the brain as it does, would contra-indicate its use. I would not use it on a patient who fears it, for it might produce cerebral anæmia, which is a condition you would not like to have. Another class of cases in which I would refrain from using it is in pregnant women.

Dr. Kester of Chicago: In what part of the anatomy of the dog were the injections made?

The Essayist: In the upper portions of the back and body, just where it was convenient. I would like to add, in this connection, that dogs under the influence of cocaine, instead of being vicious or unruly, are quiet and peaceful. The drug seems to have such a powerful effect on some of them that they are inclined to stay around you, seeming as though they wanted you to help them, and feeling as if man might be of service to them.

Dr. J. H. Martindale of Minneapolis : I notice that in a number of the cases reported by the essayist, at the autopsies there was congestion of the kidneys as well as of the lungs.

Dr. Morrison of Indianapolis: The gentleman has so thoroughly opened the discussion and so thoroughly closed it that there is nothing left to be said. He has conducted his investigations in a way that has been highly satisfactory to myself, and in a manner that is very creditable indeed. He has referred to the physiological and toxicological effects of cocaine, so that it will not be necesssary for me to dwell on that portion of the subject. I will say that in my use of the drug, I have confined myself almost exclusively to its topical effects, applying it to the gums and the surrounding tissues exclusive of the hypodermic method. I might say that in almost every case, where the rubber dam was applied, the application of cocaine has produced satisfactory results. We know when we have tight ligatures under the gums, operations are attended with pain, and cocaine in almost all of these cases reduces the pain, and in such instances I make it about as strong as it can be used. I take a bottle of the crystals, dip a little pledget of cotton in water, making almost a syrupy solution of the cocaine, and paint it around the gums before putting on the rubber dam.

Dentists sometimes get colds in the head, as is the case with myself; at such times take a mild solution of cocaine, a two or four per cent solution with a camel's hair brush and sniff up a few drops of it, this will settle the cold. It will stop it permanently. An application or two will suffice. The only bad effect that I get from its use is where it is injected hypodermically. I am always afraid of that operation. In most cases it is not necessary. If we have a bad case of extraction, I think in almost all instances the exhibition of ether or gas is far better, and less risky than the application of cocaine hypodermically. A case I had, led me to believe that in a great many instances where there was trouble from the application of cocaine hypodermically, it was due to carelessness on part of both the patient and myself. I was injecting it for the extraction of a third superior molar root, and by means of a sudden pushing forward of the head of the patient the needle went through the process I expected to inject it into, and the greater part of the solution went into the throat of the patient, and as the patient was a little susceptible to sudden frights under ordinary circumstances, you can imagine what would follow from spasmodic contraction of the muscles of the throat. It was a long time before the patient was cured. I think that in a great many cases where we have had these spasmodic contractions of the muscles of the throat, it has been due entirely to getting a few drops of the cocaine solution into the throat, and relieving the sensibility perhaps of the epiglottis, so that in the effort to swallow the patient got it down in the throat.

It is unnecessary for me to further discuss this subject, except to say that in all of these cases where we can operate on the soft tissues, I think we can get benefit from its use topically.

Dr. Martindale of Minneapolis : It has been since January, 1885, that I have been using this drug hypodermically to some extent. I have not operated on the lower animals in the way the essayist has done. We are indebted to him for his having informed us of the results of his efforts. I have made some experiments for the purpose of trying to eliminate the factor of imagination. I tried to observe the action of the drug in several instances, and indulged in doses which should have produced exhilaration. I have known of two or three cases of nausea indirectly induced by the exercise of the drug upon them, but in the majority of cases, I am sure the toxic evidences that have been manifested were largely the result of my patients assuming that I was examining them with a view to ascertaining such toxic evidences. There is one point that should be borne in mind, and that is I distrust any solutions of whatever strength that have been kept in my office more than a couple of days, either winter or summer. I have little tablets of the drug which the druggist puts up for me. I have noticed, too, that when I give my patients cold water to wash the mouth out we oftentimes have considerable soreness of the tissues after using the drug ; and in one case that I at present recall, an abscess occurred. I now use warm water and do not find any bad effects.

Dr. I. A. Freeman of Chicago : I have had a limited experience with the use of this drug. I rise more particularly for the purpose of stating some things that have occurred to me in reference to its use. Mention has been made of nausea occurring. An instance was given me not many days ago of a physician administering about one grain of the drug for a prolonged and severe attack of vomiting, which resulted in a cure of the case. While this may not prove anything, it is yet helpful to a certain extent, in that it shows different results from its use. I had a physician administer the drug hypodermically for the purpose of preparing a root for crowning. The patient was subject to hysteria, and had been under this physician's care for a considerable length of time, consequently I desired to have the matter placed in his hands where it might be safe. We very soon had a case of labored breathing, a good deal of disturbance in the region of the heart—in short, the symptoms were quite alarming, lasting about twenty minutes, when the patient became free from any distressing manifestations.

I have used it very frequently for extracting, wedging, and other operations about the mouth. I feel that we have been highly favored by the researches that Dr. Pruyn has given in this direction. He has been an enthusiast for some time upon it, and has studied the subject with great care.

Dr. Atkinson of New York:—We have had a bad experience with the drug in the East, and those of you who have read the results of Dr. Mattison's experiments know that they have been adverse to a very heavy per cent. I have seen this hilarious intoxication from cocaine that has been referred to, and to say that infirmity follows its action would transcend my reading on the subject. There is a law in the application of remedies, and if we do not understand that law, we should wait, or ask counsel. It remains in the hands of experimenters, and what may be accomplished by it we do not at present know. The history of cocaine, used as an arrester of the waste metamorphosis of tissue in certain troubles, is open to small doubt. I am decidedly disposed to say, hands off!

Dr. William Conrad of St. Louis:—This paper has given me a great deal of pleasure. The use of cocaine has been in my opinion very much abused. I have operated with it in different conditions perhaps a hundred times, and have seen no very bad results from it, but I have seen some of the symptoms mentioned, and some that have given me a little trouble, but nothing that would alarm me. I have not used less than one-fourth of a grain hypodermically. I have used as much as a grain and a half. But I must say, gentlemen, that the more I use of it, and the more I hear intelligent men talk about its use, the more careful I become. There are certain cases we meet with in the practice of dentistry, where to do the necessary operation without some form of anæsthetic would be almost out of the question. Chloroform or ether, I think, are too potent remedies for what we might term trivial operations. The use of nitrous-oxide is out of the question, because its effects do not last long enough to give the operator time to operate safely. In such cases I would recommed the use of cocaine, mixed at the time of using, and the mixture I use is that recommended by Viau, of France. I had used it quite frequently without adding carbolic acid, as recommended by this gentleman, and my results were not satisfactory. With the use of the carbolic acid solution, I have had much satisfaction in removing deeply embedded teeth. In removing embedded wisdom teeth, in removing teeth where there is irregularity, it is almost impossible to reach them rapidly; in these cases I would suggest its use.

The essayist, in closing the discussion, said: My friend Dr. Martindale speaks of its decomposition; that keeping it in the office for a few days renders it unfit for use. He may avoid that by adding to his solution salicylic or carbolic acid, or any of the other antifermentative agents that are in use. I prefer salicylic acid, and very few grains of it will keep the solution for days. In some instances the solution will be good for months after the first use.

Dr. Freeman, while he is not a homœopath, alludes to the fact of cocaine being used for the control of vomiting. I am not a homeopathist, but still the fact of a remedy acting as it does shows that there may be something in it. I think, however, that there are many drugs besides cocaine that I would rather use to prevent vomiting.

There were a few points in the paper that, I think, were not made sufficiently clear to some of you, and one of them was in what cases would I refrain from using it. I should be inclined to prohibit its use in cases of heart trouble, whether it involves the valves of the heart or any other portion of the organ. If this remedy has such an effect upon the circulation and respiration, as some claim it does, we should refrain from using it. We should prohibit its use in cases of disease of the kidneys. I would not use it in the case of a pregnant woman. Dr. Atkinson says it is an unreliable drug; that it never acts just the same. While all drugs are uncertain as far as their therapeutical action is concerned, this drug seems to be more uncertain than any other with which I am acquainted. While we are using it with success, Dr. Atkinson urges us to be careful in its use. In handling it have at your hand all known remedies for resuscitation in case a toxic condition should develop. If you have children to deal with, the doses should be proportionate to their age, and I find I can get all the toxic effects I want from small doses carefully used. I find it a valuable remedy, but, like many other good things, it can be abused.

Dr. Templeton of Pittsburg: Have you ever used it in the case of very young children?

The essayist: I have used it in young children, and in most cases they bear it with greater tolerance in proportion to their age than older people.

The President than announced that clinics would commence at the Chicago College of Dental Surgery promptly at 9 o'clock, Wednesday morning, February 6.

On motion the society adjourned till 7:30 P. M.

EVENING SESSION.

The society re-convened at 7:30 P. M., and was called to order by the President.

Dr. J. J. R. Patrick of Belleville, Illinois, contributed a paper entitled:

THE STUDY OF PRE-HISTORIC REMAINS IN THEIR RELATION TO DENTISTRY.

Some fifty-nine years ago, under the direction of the Canal Commisioners of Illinois, James Thompson surveyed and platted the small town of Chicago; he was for many years afterward County Judge of Randolph County. At the time of the survey, the Pottawattamie Indians owned 20,000,000 acres of land in this region, including Cook County, which they ceded to the Government, and were moved west of the Mississippi. Many years prior to the permanent settlement of this region, by an English-speaking people, the shores of this lake were visited by the celebrated Frenchmen, Marquette, Joliet, Hennepin and LaSalle. When these pious pioneers, in 1673, visited the site of the now great city of Chicago, the Tamaroas and Pottawattamies roamed over this vast region undisturbed by the European.

If our rude predecessors could arise from their graves and revisit the theater of their earthly career, and see the country in its present condition, it is doubtful whether they would have sufficient intelligence to be surprised. The growth of large cities, packed with industrious people, occupying their abandoned lands; multitudes of domestic cattle, supplanting the wild herds of buffalo and deer; machinery resembling organic beings in delicacy of structure; the powers of matter applied to give motion to that machinery; speedy locomotion by land and water, supplanting the pack and the canoe; illumination and the transmission of intelligence—in short, the civilizations of the old world, transplanted in the new, taking deep root and making vigorous growth, are so far removed from the conceptions of the savages to whom I have alluded, that they could not be expected to look on such progress with intelligent wonder.

On the other hand, it can be said with equal truth that if the great mass of humanity that has supplanted the savage, presenting as they do all the outward appearance of civilization, were asked to explain the means by which they arrived at such a condition—the many sources from which they draw their wardrobe, or adornment, the many channels through which civilization furnishes their breakfast table—it is doubtful if they would have sufficient knowledge of the workings or the make-up of civilization to give an intelligent answer. The Indian, receiving his blanket from the Government, and the civilized man, receiving his garments from the hands of his tailor, are almost equally unconscious of the many processes through which the material passes in the course of manfacture.

This great progress has all been effected little by little, at times more rapidly than at others, but, viewing the whole course of civilization, it has been gradual, though moving with an accelerated ratio. The explanation of so rapid a progress is to be found in the constantly increasing division and subdivision of labor, building up the social fabric in the same manner that special cells compose and build up each part of a living organism; and it is a wise provision in nature that each division and subdivision in labor, each segmentation in the cellular formation of living organisms, is dependent on the other, and is the outgrowth from natural law. If we review the history of the sciences, we shall find that marked advance has been made in a given science only when it has been connected with the progress of some collateral science or art. Thus, the astronomer when connected with the optician, was capable of rapid progress. It was known for centuries that a piece of steel, rubbed against a piece of peculiar mineral, had the power of attracting iron; and amber, if rubbed, had the temporary power of attracting light substances; but these phenomena were only deemed exceptional.

Time finally brought the theorist and machinist together, and what are now the triumphs of magnetism and electricity? It would be out of place here, and treating of matters too familiar to my audience, to show how much we are indebted to the refinements of chemical analysis for our knowledge of the elementary constitution of the earthy salts that enter into the composition of the hard tissues of the body; or to the important facts revealed by the use of the microscope to the science of physiology, together with the creation of the science of animal morphology, brought about by investigations into the cellular structure of plants. It is very clear that if the practical man had no time at his disposal, and the theoretic one lacked that skill in manipulation requisite to give the appropriate degree of excellence to the material with which to experiment, advance in the proper direction would be for the time impeded.

The superiority of the civilized over the savage man is in proportion to the extent to which his thought can grasp the past and the future. His memory reaches further back; his capability of prediction reaches further forward, in proportion as his knowledge increases. He realizes that it is not altogether what he sees, but how he sees; he critically examines what he has seen, and recognizes the objects that are of importance. The senses, he has learned, are merely the substructure for the grandest systems of thought, and in their development must be subject to the action of the culture to which they give rise. In uncultivated minds, the senses are the teachers; but in cultivated minds they are led by the understanding. A weak, but disciplined, eye can see more objects than the strong but undisciplined one—for it discovers truth from so many sides, so necessary in scientific inquiry. In short, when the eye is controlled by the understanding, it is capable of distinguishing what is new and valuable from the hackneyed and worthless; it is never thrown out of focus by chimeras, but receives the impress of objects truthfully, or, if the eye is defective by nature, or enfeebled by age, the understanding corrects the error, or restores the enfeebled eye to usefulness.

There can be no question in regard to the division of labor being the main principle in the civilization of mankind, and that specialties in scientific pursuits have been the cause of their great advancement. But when specialties in scientific pursuits, or labor in the useful arts, become narrowed down or restricted to a few principles, they become subversive of mental exertion, and can not fail to produce disastrous results. Specialties in science must have a dependence upon universal knowledge to exist, for, as the earth is illuminated by celestial bodies by night and day, so any specialty, either in the arts or sciences, must constantly receive the light from other sciences and other arts to be in concert.

The practice of dentistry and surgery has a history as old as medicine, and medicine, as we all know, is as old as disease itself; but these professions remained for many centuries in a passive condition, until they received a progressive impulse from the mind of John Hunter. Blot out the original investigations and discoveries of this great laborer in the field of original research, and these three professions would be in the condition they were when he found them—largely in the hands of quacks and charlatans. Now, it is not altogether the work that Hunter performed himself, but the exact methods of investigation that he introduced, which gave a new and vigorous impetus to scientific research in every department.

From these considerations it is clear that a specialty, to be in the van of progress, must not only receive, but give, for in this consists the law of progress.

When we pass to the consideration of the rapid advance our own specialty has made of late years, we must attribute it largely to the growth of associations, for the advantages conferred by these societies are manifold ; they enable those who are devoted to scientific research to combine, compare and check their observations, to assist, by the thoughts of several minds, the promotion of any inquiry undertaken. They afford a means of submitting to a competent tribunal, essays or memoirs, and of obtaining for their authors, or others, by means of the discussions that follow, information from those well-informed on the particular subject. They contribute from a joint purse to such efforts as their members deem most worthy, and defray the expense of printing and publishing such researches as are thought meritorious. Societies thus organized are co-operative in their character, and are a powerful means in the promotion of progress.

But a society composed exclusively of one profession, unfortunately, has a tendency to contract upon itself, to show undue respect for the authority of superficial collectors of information, and to follow blindly the work of others, without regard to verification. A society thus restricted in its methods will unconsciously foster an antipathy to the minute details of scientific research, and encourage methods of investigation that are generally diffusive in their character.

Now, there are questions brought before our societies, from time to time, for solution, that are treated in a diffusive manner, that could, and should be treated or investigated by more exact methods. I refer to those questions that involve the comparative frequency of diseases of the teeth of the savage and the civilized man.

Are there any influences connected with civilization that are productive of degeneracy of the dental system ? Is civilization to be charged with the frequent anomalies to be met with in the civilized man ? Is decay of the teeth peculiar to civilization ? Now, it is very clear that these questions can not be answered intelligently, until the following question is answered : Are the dental systems of uncivilized races of men free from anomalies, and all those diseases and malformations of the oral cavity so common to the civilized ?

If we refer these questions to the general practitioner of either medicine or dentistry, the answer will be that the savage is exempt from these diseases and malformations, and that civilized man, owing to his artificial mode of living, requires artificial methods to support his organism ; that while his mental capacity has increased, it has been at the expense of his physical. When asked for proof of these statements, we are met with generalities ; statistics some- times are quoted, but only from the side of civilization. Now, see- ing that the savage has no asylums to investigate, no physicians or dentists to interrogate, that we could recognize as reliable, and no sta- tistics to question, the conclusions drawn are quite *natural*, and being natural, are one-sided and very savage, but certainly not scientific.

Had the question of civilization being the cause of tooth decay never been introduced for discussion, the practitioner of dentistry could have saved decayed teeth, and corrected deformities, without troubling himself about the condition of the mouth of the savage. Yea, he could have investigated the cause of disease, and irregularity of development, equally as well in the organism of the civilized man, without the least reference to the condition of the organism of the savage, and there is no doubt in my mind that if the savage had been allowed to rest in peace, so far as this question is concerned, there would have been more truly scientific workers in the field of inquiry as to the origin of diseases and malformations of the human mouth.

As the question now stands, the savage is an important factor in the inquiry, and if, upon investigation, it is found that he is not the physically perfect creature he has been represented to be, then this driftwood that has in all probability been drawn from tradition, or the archives of the imagination, and that has dammed up the stream of our professional progress, will be swept away to the gulf of ob- livion. If this should be proven to be the case, there would be less opportunity for differences of opinion in regard to the condition of the teeth and jaws of the savage and the civilized; much valuable time would be saved in our society meetings in the discussion of dietary methods of reconstructing or rejuvenating the human teeth, and the time thus saved could be devoted to the subjects of digestion and assimilation, with a probability of more profit.

It is fortunate for the solution of this subject that the inquiry is restricted to the hard and least destructible portions of the body, as cicatrices or cysts, the result of lesions by disease during life, anomalies or decay may be readily recognized. And as the science of geology teaches the history of our globe during immense periods of time, revealing to the mind vestiges of animal and vegetable forms which have appeared and disappeared, leaving their fossil remains in successively deposited strata, forming an indelible history; so the remains of pre-historic men are, in point of certainty, for the consideration of the anomalies and diseases of his jaws and teeth, as true a guide as the fossils are to the geologist in reconstructing the history of the earth. A number of these records exist in our museums, while thousands lie buried in the soil, much as we find the remains of former life entombed in the strata of the earth.

If these remains are examined, the forms of the crowns of the teeth and their roots could be noted; whether the crowns carried supplemental or multiple tubercles; whether convergence or divergence of the roots prevailed; augmentation or *geantism*, in whole or part, and the relative volume; diminution, or *nanism* of the teeth; augmentation or diminution on one or both sides of the arches; malposition by crowding; malposition by transposition; displacement of permanent by deciduous teeth outside the arch, or in the vault of the palate; inclusion of teeth in the jaw; confusion and fusion; transversion and reversion; anteversion and retroversion in whole or part; lateral constriction of the arches; rotation of single teeth on their axes; rotation by imbrication; erosion, grooved, pitted, granular or crescentic; odontomes of cementum, of enamel, and diffused; supernumerary teeth fused to permanent, and their position; partial division of the crowns of teeth; asymetry of the arches; diastema, double or single; augmentation of the transverse diameter of the arches; atrophy of the jaws, right or left, and caries of the teeth—these are some of the diseases and anomalies of the teeth and jaws that civilized humanity is afflicted with.

It is impossible to know what might be revealed in a physiological and pathological point of view in regard to the dental system of pre-historic man, until his remains are examined and tabulated. I respectfully and earnestly invite cooperative investigation on the subject. It is one of great importance to the profession, which will grow in interest as the investigation progresses, while at the present time it remains in comparative obscurity.

DISCUSSION.

Before proceeding with the discussion on Dr. Patrick's paper the Chair announced that Dr. E. M. S. Fernandez of Chicago, would give a clinic February the sixth, at the College, in which he would demonstrate his method of filling with the oxyphosphates and oxychlorides.

Dr. E. T. Darby of Philadelphia, was selected to open the discussion, but was absent.

The Chair seeing Dr. H. J. McKellops, called upon him, who on rising, said: "Mr. President, I have nothing particular to say on this subject, but some years ago if you remember, I offered a resolution in the American Dental Association at Cincinnati, for the appropriation of money to investigate and tabulate the skulls in charge of the Surgeon General of the United States. There has not been a particle of work done in that matter. It stands to-day where it was then, and the reason the paper is read is to show the want of such investigations. There is a field for work in this direction, and what we need is to appropriate an amount sufficient to thoroughly investigate the subject.

Dr. Atkinson was called for. He said: I have only to commend the wisdom of the writer of the paper in taking the ground he did. It is unfortunate that we have had no investigations made on such an important and interesting subject. I agree with the essayist and Dr. McKellops' expression of the necessity of making all the observations possible within the available reach of scientific research.

The President, noticing that Dr. Darby had just entered the room, called upon him to participate in the discussion. Dr. Darby ascended the platform. He said: "Mr. President and Gentlemen, I am very sorry not to have been here on time as expected, but I accepted the invitation of a friend to dinner, hence am a little late. I do not know that I have anything valuable to say upon the subject under discussisn. I have always read with interest everything that Dr. Patrick has written upon the subject of dentistry. He kindly gave me his paper to look over, so that I might be prepared to say something on the subject. I must acknowledge I read it hastily, so that I did not get the full sense of the paper nor the work which he presented. But I infer from a casual glance at the paper that its object was more to encourage careful observation on the part of the profession in this work than anything else. It is true that we know something of the character of the teeth of the ancients, but we do not know how careful they were with them. The subject has been one to which I have given

some considerable attention, and one which I am exceedingly
interested in at present, because some of my studies at the
present time have been in the direction or line of Dr. Patrick's
paper.

Some years ago it was a pleasure to look personally into this
matter of the teeth of the ancients. I not only read upon the subject very extensively, but gave it a good deal of thought and study.
It has been said that the ancients suffered less, and perhaps not at
all, from diseases of the teeth than we of to-day. We know, however, from the remains that have been found in the ancient tombs
of Tuscany that they suffered from some of the conditions which
we find at the present day. It is an old story, and a true one, that
deterioration is following the centuries as we go onward in time,
but that is not true in all parts. I should be sorry if men of the
present day were not as robust, either physically, or as well-devel-
oped mentally, as centuries ago. My observations in the East, in
Egypt, the Holy Land, and other places, wherever I had opportunities of examining the teeth of the ancients, were that they seemed
to have been in better condition, though my observations were not
extensive enough for me to speak authoritatively. I had unusual
opportunities in Egypt for examining the teeth of the ancients at
the time I was there; the mummy pits, which were then under the
supervision of a Frenchman, who was locked up during the siege
of Paris, offered a splendid opportunity for study. I went into
these mummy pits, and dug them out with my hands, one after
another, extracting the teeth of the ancient mummies as they had
been embalmed, and carefully examining them, and with but a single exception did I find a tooth missing, and in only two exceptional instances did I find evidences of carious teeth. These
mummies were placed in the pits no less than three or four thous-
and years ago, before there was evidence of this method of em-
balming—going back to the time of Abraham and the great Pyra-
mid of Cheops. I also had opportunities of examining the teeth of
the ancients at the Convent of Saint Katherine, at Mount Sinai, in
the charnel house. Every monk that has died or dies has his
skull and all his bones placed in this charnel house. I got permission of one of the monks to go into the charnel house and examine
these skulls, but of course my examinations were not made with
care—that is, they were not tabulated. I might say, also, that
these skulls were arranged in the order of the centuries in which

the monks died.   I went through these tombs, examined a great many teeth, and with very few exceptions did I find decay; it was only in skulls dated three or four centuries back that I found decay to any considerable extent.   So I was led to suppose, from my observations in the Egyptian mummy pits, that the teeth of the mummies in the various museums at that time or generation were vastly poorer than those of the ancient Egyptians.   I found, also, that the teeth of the Egyptians of the present day were better than ours, and the Bedouins or Arabs of the Desert had vastly better teeth than those who lived in cities and subsisted on an entirely different kind of food, which consisted largely of the phosphates. I found that the Arabs lived mostly upon barley bread baked in the ashes, beans, etc.   They rarely ever touched animal food. It was the rarest thing that these Arabs had anything to eat except the bread they baked in the ashes; and their teeth were, almost without exception, good.

I went, also, into the desert of Sahara, and found that the Saharans or Arabs of Sahara had poorer teeth than the Egyptians or Bedouins of Santiac, for they lived upon a food largely of an animal nature, and less upon those kinds of food which contain the phosphates.   Yet all these data do not prove to us that the teeth of previous generations were so very much poorer than our own.

Dr. Thompson of Topeka called attention to the fact that some years ago he brought out the idea that the teeth of man were in process of suppression in the race, which attracted a great deal of attention ; and to-day we know that the wisdom tooth is in process of suppression ; no dentist would deny that.   We know also that some of the other teeth sometimes disappear or fail to appear.   He had listened with pleasure to the remarks of the previous speakers, and thought that investigations looking toward the accomplishment of the object in view should be carried out.

Dr. Sudduth of Philadelphia : I have never had opportunities of investigation in this direction, but it seems to me it is a shame that the dental profession should be satisfied with such a superficial view of this question.   Much valuable time has been given to discussions on papers upon the influence of diet and civilization upon decay of the teeth without any just basis upon which to work. It appears to me that right here in Illinois where we have evidences in the pre-historic mounds, that the societies and dentists of this State should have taken more active steps than they have to investigate and tabulate data upon which to reason in regard to this work.   The point brought out by Dr. Patrick was the necessity of special observation and tabulation in regard to the question under consideration.   We ought to take hold of the subject, and enable some men capable of making these investigations to bring out a work that will be a credit to the dental profession.   This point was brought out at a meeting of the Illinois State Dental Society at its meeting in Quincy some years ago, and a committee was appointed, but so far as I know it has died in the committee.   I have never heard or read any report from it.   What we need is reliable data upon which to base our observations.   The more I attend dental meetings the more deeply I am impressed with the utilitarian aspect of American character, and as was said by Dr. Patrick, we want broad, comprehensive discussions on papers.   We want specialties within specialties in order to get at the basal facts of these things.   We can not expect to advance as a profession in original investigations on nothing; it takes time and money, and the men selected to carry out this work must be supported.

Dr. J. N. Crouse of Chicago :   I want to defend myself in this matter.   I believe I was the chairman of the committee alluded to. The matter was brought before the American Dental Association, at Cincinnati, with a view to getting the co-öperation of dentists all over the country, and somebody said there was a scheme in that to get ahead of somebody else, and that killed it.

Dr. Patrick, in closing the discussion, said: We want stubborn, irresistible facts that can be referred to.   The evidence must come in before the verdict is rendered.   The object of the paper was not to inform you how many decayed teeth there were in an Indian skull.   I kept away from him.   It is not my business to show you the benefits that may be derived from an investigation of this sub- ject.   As I stated particularly in my paper, the subject may have slipped your recognition, and that it is one-sided until it is investi- gated, and the Indian has come to stay.   You cannot get rid of him. Just so long as a man can make an Indian a scape-goat to explain the disease of civilization, he will do it ; he will never investigate them.   That is the reason why I said the savage man ought not to be in the question ; we would have got along better without him. The past history of dentistry is imperfect; so it is of medicine.   Not until investigations are made of pre-historic remains and tabulated by one gentleman and another will we accomplish the desired result.

CARIES AND NECROSIS IN THEIR RELATION TO PRACTICAL DENTISTRY.

By J. H. MARTINDALE, M.D., D.D.S., Minneapolis, Minn.

In being permitted this evening to invite your attention to the subject suggested by your committee, "Caries and Necrosis of the Jaws and Alveolar Structures," I do so with knowledge that I shall be unable to present anything very new or valuable as to the etiology or management of these conditions which, although highly important, consist of a topical and systemic treatment which, for the last few years, has changed very little. I trust, however, that as long as the established truisms of medical science with respect to caries and necrosis are so comparatively little understood and practiced as at present, you will excuse me if my treatise presents very little of scientific hypothesis or surmise.

Before we can intelligently consider caries or necrosis as an affection of the jaws and alveolar structures, we must first consider it as affecting osseous tissues in general. In a pathological sense, diseases of the bones are identical with those of other tissues, while such differences as exist are due to their anatomical and physiological peculiarities, diseased action under all conditions being materially modified by texture. In the bones diseased action is thus modified by the presence of the inorganic material which they contain, two-thirds of their constituents being earthy and one-third animal.

This animal proportion of the texture of the bones includes a fibrous periosteal membrane with cellular tissue beneath; and in the long bones of an endosteum or inner periosteum, which lines their medullary canals. With this latter class of bones this paper has no concern, hence the subject of osteo-myelitis, or the "inflammation of the bone marrow," as Thomas Bryant designates it, although a subject of the most intense importance and interest to the general or orthopædic surgeon, will not be touched upon here.

Caries, or necrosis of the jaws and alveoli, always point to an antecedent condition of inflammation, although it by no means follows that inflammation of the jawbone has, as a necessary sequella, caries or necrosis of the same. As inflammation can only pertain to vital animal substances, the process of inflammation in bone can be found only in that organic vital plasma so inexplicably and mysteriously blended with minerals to form the bony tissues of the animal organism. In the jaws this substance is found in the periosteum, the bone cells, and the inosculating of their canaliculli, and in the circulatory system of the Haversian canals. With the tangled net-work of fact and hypothesis that at present constitutes our acquaintance with the subject of inflammation, it is unnecessary that I should here burden you. Let it suffice to say that when inflammation of this highly vascular periosteum has been induced in the maxillæ or alveola appendages thereof, by traumatism, septic infection, cachexia, or by specific mineral poisons, and proceeding through the successive stages of increase of blood to the part, multiplication of leucocytes and congestion, finally reaches complete stasis, so that nutrition from a definite and considerable area of bone is suddenly cut off, *necrosis* must then inevitably result. If, on the contrary, complete arrest or capillary infarction shall not have been reached, but the blood current has been slowed, and the interstitial portions of bone have become the seat of foreign elements and the scene of perverted nutrition, we reach the stage so admirably described by Dr. Ingersoll, whom I now quote.

Speaking of the transudation occurring in congestion, he says : "Red corpuscles follow the white, but not in such large numbers. Stagnant blood in which the corpuscles are dead also passes out. From the damage done to the vascular tissue, and to the contiguous cellular tissue, there is a debris left to mingle in the flood of disorganized material which constitutes pus. In addition to the matter which is the result of the disorganization of tissue, there is, according to modern discoveries, a large emigration from without, in form of micro-organisms of various types, considered to be exopathic causes in the formative processes of developing pus." Professor Dalton, in his physiology, tells us that this intercellular or interstitial area which we see by Dr. Ingersoll's apt description has now become the field of such strained conditions and anomalous elements, in the *normal* state of circulation is filled with interstitial fluid, which is the source of nutriment for the solid parts surrounding it, and is renewed by constant change. As fresh supplies are drawn from the circulating blood, the older portions are removed by absorption and returned to the center of circulation by the lymphatic vessels. Now, if the condition described has been reached, we find that the interstitial area of bone so affected presents a very chaotic mixture, embryonic cells, blood corpuscles, dead blood cells, and the debris of the tissue involved in the inflammation. We have present as you see *re*-constructive and *de*structive elements we are viewing the ultimate battle ground of tissues. In proportion now to the *natural vital force*, of the human subject in whom these changes are taking place, and his predispositions of ca-chexia, we view either the wonderful upbuilding of molecular form of new tissues, or tissue death, molecule by molecule being cast off with pus in the form of dead bone-earth ; this we call *caries* of bone. If I succeed to any degree in differentiating the causes and progress of caries and necrosis, it is perhaps the most valuable purpose this paper could possibly subserve.   The terms, as I know, are too often used by dentists interchangeably and with very loose conceptions of what really constitute their respective distinctions.   No doubt necrosed areas of bone are often found in connection with caries, and as a result of the progress of that disease, having insulated as it were small territories of bone, and by thus cutting off their blood supply causing necrosis.   According to the definitions in the books *necrosis* is a condition analagous to gangrene, or slough in the soft parts, and *caries* is described as a condition of the bones similar to that of ulcerations in the soft parts, with the exception that the disintegrated bone-tissue contains bone earth, and this debris acts as an irritant in the tissues, exciting the florid granulations which grow so plentifully from the surface of a sore, or fistula over a por-tion of carious bone.   Caries presents a spectacle similar to that of a well-contested battle-ground where life and death are closely con-tiguous.   Here a molecule yields, dies, and is carried off in the tor-rent of pus and death waste, and right beside it is a healthy mole-cule waging valiant defense against the usurper.   In necrosis, to the contrary, the defending forces, represented in bone as we have previously stated by the lacunæ, their canaliculi, and the Haver-sian system of vessels, find themselves like besieged soldiers in a barracks sorely oppressed by the enemy, their sources of nourish-ment from without having been commpletely cut off; they surren-der the barracks en masse, and leave it dead and tenantless—a mere mass of mineral matter like the coral in the museum, once the abiding place of animal life, now an empty skeleton."

Holmes says in his system of surgery, " When a portion of bone is to die, the first phenomenon is the cessation of circulation in it.   This leaves it hard, white, and sonorous when struck.   It does not bleed when exposed or cut into, and is insensible."   It is very frequently the case, that the periosteum immediately covering the area of bone thus necrosed is lifted up by an effusion of inflammatory products, but instead of dying, its bone producing cells being irritated to an excessive activity, proliferate a film of bone which encloses or invaginates the dead bone, requiring that we should cut and penetrate this new bone e'er we remove that which is dead beneath it. In the lower jaw also, which as you know consists of an outer and an inner plate, which are of very dense and compact osseous tissue, enclosing a cancellous portion, these plates, especially the external plate, are bulged out by the inflammatory effusions beneath, forming a tumor appearance which when pressed will frequently be found to be so thin that it will very readily yield beneath the finger — I, in my practice, very frequently find this condition presenting as a result of acute inflammations of the bone resulting in effusion. Later on if resolution does not occur said effusions will form for themselves an outlet and this bulged out plate of bone will collapse. In other instances the effusions being capable of organization into new products, the cavity becomes filled with dense bone, and a permanent bony tumor is the result. Having attempted thus far to trace pathologically the progress and nature of these diseases as presented in the maxillary bones, let us now enquire into some of those blood taints or cachexia which especially predispose to, or directly cause Necrosis and Caries — among them are the exanthematous diseases common especially to childhood (measles, scarlet fever, chicken pox, etc). In them exfoliation of a considerable portion of the alveolar process involving the deciduous teeth therein contained, and even the follicles of the permanent ones is by no means uncommon; especially does it follow measles, commencing subsequently to the active stage of the disease, in tenderness of the gums, fetid breath, but no severe inflammatory action, the gums recede from the teeth, and bare bone is exposed, this exfoliates, and leaves a gap in the jaw, which is gradually filled up with new bone. Of late years the attention of the writer is being more and more called to the prevalence of caries and necrosis as a result of inflammation aroused by traumatism, or other means, in the bones of scrofulous persons, or those of tubercular diathesis. In such cases modern authorities tell us, the cell proliferation which is the natural consequence of the inflammation resulting from a contusion of the tissues, in place of quickly taking on a reparative action, has a tendency to hyperplasia reverting to embryonic conditions and so to a nesting or bunching of cells such as is often met with in the medulla of bone in tubercular affections of the osseous system ; the reversions to an embryonic type, are *apparent* only, as these cells are doomed in the majority of cases to death and degeneration. Cases of this kind have several times presented themselves in my practice, and later on I shall quote some of them in detail from my case book.

Constitutional syphilis is a predisposing condition to necrosis, and such a case as that cited by Sir Christopher Heath, in his work on " Diseases of the Jaws," where a dentist had suit brought against him for a case of necrosis, ensuing as the result of an extraction of a tooth, the patient being a syphilite, is not uncommon. A large number of the cases, however, which are usually ascribed to syphilis probably are induced by the great amount of mercury and iodide of potassium, which are the drugs so extensively used in its treatment. No inconsiderable number of diseased skulls and other bones to be found in our museums, exhibit the results of mercurial poisoning. Mahomedans and Hindoos, in various parts of Hindostan, believe that mercury is a specific for fever and for that purpose it is given in a most reckless manner, with the result of inducing extensive necrosis of the skull and other bones. Especially when used so freely as is even now in our own country so common by inunction, we may not infrequently witness symptoms simulating those of secondary syphilis, but which are really due to excessive mercurialization of the system.

The writer himself has a patient who assures him that when a few years ago at the Hot Springs he was treated most heroically for syphilis by inunction; he could frequently discover little globules of free mercury in the creases in the palms of his hands, and coins carried in his pockets at that time were silvered over with a mercuric amalgam.

McNamara, in his work upon the bones, states that mercury has been found in its free metalic state in the bones, and thinks that by blocking up the small vessels and canals of the osseous tissues, it so interferes with the circulation of a part as to result in death of the bone. Necrosis of the alveolus during the administration of mercury, however, may occur from a different cause, depending upon the condition of the gums through which the supply of blood to the bone is largely supplied. If profuse salivation exists, the ulcerating and sloughing condition of the gums must largely interfere with the flow of blood to the alveoli of both upper and lower jaws ; and so the occurrence of necrosis of bone in this locality is explained precisely as we see in cases of cancrum oris. Another mineral poison with specific tendencies to effect necrosis of the jaws is phosphorus, the fumes of which inhaled by workmen in match factories, induce the most extensive necrosis, the remarkable feature being that through some peculiar affinity existing between the poison and tooth pulps exposed by decay, the workmen are said to breathe the phosphorus fumes with comparative immunity as relates to necrosis if only their teeth are free from decay or kept properly filled. But of the foregoing disease, as it is of very infrequent occurrence in this part of the country, we shall treat no further in this paper.

We come now to the causes most prolific of caries and necrosis in the jaws, and alveolus, especially as encountered in dental practice, namely, traumatism—blows, kicks, bruises and the like, which are frequent causes, especially when occurring in individuals of scrofulous or strumous habit. A great many, undoubtedly the larger number, of diseased conditions of the maxillæ originate in diseases of the teeth or their sockets, and in ill-advised or careless dental operations. Among the former may be enumerated dead tooth pulps, encysted teeth, and delayed eruption of the wisdom teeth. And among the latter, heavy malleting, roots improperly filled and roots filled with improper filling (as cotton unimpregnated with any preservative medicine).

The writer has also frequently had occasion to note (once he regrets to say in his own early practice), *necrosis* (never caries), as a result of the application of arsenious acid for the purpose of effecting devitalization of the dental pulp, said application having been insufficiently well sealed from the fluids of the mouth. To the relief of the dental surgeon be it stated that eminent authorities unite in saying, (and the writer's observation in practice also persuade him to the belief), that in addition to the cases of diseased maxillæ, the unquestioned result of cachexia, exanthemata, mineral poisons and traumatism, many cases occur which are without doubt idiopathic.

Emphasis is placed upon this fact, in consequence of the too frequent reproach cast upon skilled and discreet dental surgeons, that their ill-advised or rough operations have induced the disease. The writer maintains that in certain cases the tissues adjacent to the field of dental operations, are in a condition peculiarly ready to take on an inflammation, which becoming an ostitis, then breaks down (in the manner described in the first part of this paper) into a veritable necrosis or caries. It should therefore be continually borne in mind that in many cases, which we are powerless to foresee, improper treatment of pulp canals, or improper filling, excessive or violent wedging, heavy malleting, and the like, may induce caries or necrosis.

Diagnosis.—In the outset, the indications that precede necrosis and caries, are not to be distinguished from maxillary or alveolar periostitis, and it is at *this* period that the timely and heroic use of the bistoury, cutting freely through the tissues down to the bone will often avert further disease—but *progressing*, instead of confining itself to local or circumscribed swelling, the gums become congested and swollen over a considerable area, and pus oozes from the margins of the gums, the teeth become loose, and in a few weeks the alveolus or maxillary plates also become disintegrated by a carious process; or necrosing, they lie dead and sequestrated, bathed in pus. Pain is common in the early part of the disease, and is usually supposed to be tooth-ache ; the patient's health often suffers greatly, symptoms of septicæmia, high temperature, sweats, rigors, etc., being frequently present.

Treatment.—All loose roots that cannot be made useful by the attachment to them of artificial crowns should be extracted. If, upon careful examination with a probe, we find that the bone is not diseased very extensively, that is, if caries has not extended further than the immediate surrounding of the roots of one or two teeth, absorption and extrusion of dead bone may usually be effected by the use of sulphuric acid brought directly in contact with the area of diseased bone. The preparation of the acid that I prefer is that known as the "Aromatic Sulphuric Acid " (a thirteen and a half per cent solution of the sulphuric acid of commerce, together with the aromatic principles of various spices). My method of using it is to inject it through the fistulous opening and directly in contact with the diseased bone by means of a hypodermic syringe, provided with a blunt ended needle, keeping it there for several minutes. I commence with a strength of about 70 per cent solution of the acid, and soon increase it to full strength. This treatment, conjoined with the use of injections of the peroxide of hydrogen, the patient's health at the same time being toned up with tonics, and the bowels being kept freely opened by the use of saline waters and aperients, will often effectually remedy the trouble. But in some instances the diseased bone is not gradually consumed

and cast off, but either large sequestra are exfoliated, needing surgical assistance in their removal, or a considerable area of honeycombed carious bone is formed, needing removal by other means
than by the dissolving properties of the acid. My treatment of
such conditions will be set forth more in detail in the recital of a
few cases from my own practice. It should be remembered, as
formerly stated in this paper, that the termination of a periostitis
in a carious or necrotic condition may often be averted if commenced early enough by freely and deeply scarifying the gums, use
of saline cathartics, rest, attention to diet, tonics, etc.

CASES.

Case 1. In February of 1882, a young boy of 19 years of age
was brought to me by his father for a condition of fixation of the
jaw, accompanied by a large swelling of the right cheek and
enlargement of the lymphatics in the cervical and sub-maxillary
region. The circumstance of extensive cicatrices upon the face,
resulting in consequent contraction of the facial muscles and dis-
torted features, immediately induced me to ask of his father the
cause, and I was informed that the boy was effected seriously with
scrofula, and that these were the result of several running sores on
the face.

As the abscess (for such it was) upon his face was already
pointed, and I could not reach it in the mouth to void its contents
there, I lanced externally and very fetid, greenish-yellow pus was
copiously poured forth. Upon closely examining this pus I found
therein contained small spiculæ of bone, and upon exploring
the abcess tract with a silver probe, I was easily able to discern the
presence of an opening in the inferior maxillary bone, just anterior
to its junction with the ascending ramus. There seemed to be no
large sequestra of bone detected by the probe, but rather a honeycombed or porous feel to the walls of the sinus. The abscess
cavity was very thoroughly irrigated with carbolized water, and
the boy was sent home with instructions to take a tonic of iron and
quinia and good nutritious food, and return in two days. It should
be remarked that the patient had been having high evening temper-
atures for several days, and his general condition was much run
down by pus absorption.

Upon his appearance at my office in two days, I found my
patient with the abscess still discharging (I had placed a seton in
the opening), but the enlarged condition of his face very much

decreased. I was now able, by the aid of a wedge and anæsthesia, to get his mouth open, and the evidence of the origin of his trouble (combined with the scrofulous cachexia) was soon evident; a late and difficult erupting wisdom tooth. Said tooth was lodged, with its masticating surface presented, in apposition to the posterior approximal surface of the second molar in front of it, and only one cusp emerging above the gums, which were very turgid and inflamed. With a physic forceps I managed to extract the offending tooth, and was then able to run my probe into the socket, and from there to the diseased tract in the maxillary bone, and so on out through the opening in the face which I had previously made.

I now had what I wanted, through drainage, and it was easy for me to inject my carbolized or other antiseptic fluids (we had not then peroxide of hydrogen at our command), through the whole diseased tract. My treatment now was a thorough scraping of the walls of the tract, with a dull scraping instrument, thorough and frequent irrigation with antiseptic washes, and a tonic treatment of the system with good food, iron, wine and quinia. After five or six days, the pus ceased to run, and in three or four days more the external wound was allowed to heal. The boy's health was renewed and the case dismissed.

Case II. I was called by a dentist, Dr. X., to see a case that had developed an undoubted carious or necrotic character. The patient was a lady aged about thirty-five years, and reported herself as possessing usually good health. Upon examination of her mouth it was seen that pus was escaping copiously from the gums surrounding the superior left central, lateral canine and first bicuspid. This condition had supervened not very long after the insertion of a not very large approximal filling in the lateral, but the circumstances were not of such a character as to suggest the probability of the filling being the direct cause, but seemed to point rather to its being one of those previously alluded to in this paper, whose origin can be ascribed to no direct source. For five or six weeks she had been subjected to the customary proper treatment with the sulphuric acid, the disease seeming not to abate, but rather to grow worse. The patient's health, also, had begun to suffer materially, her temperature running to 104, and she was generally weak and run down. Acid treatment having failed, it was a question as to what should next be done. Upon examining the parts with a probe, it was easy to determine the presence of much diseased bone and several detached pieces. The central, lateral and canine were so loose that it seemed as though it would be easy to remove them with the fingers, while the first bicuspid had begun to be seriously affected. After careful examination it was deemed best to operate for removal of the dead bone, which was done as follows:

The patient anæsthetized, holes were drilled into the pulp cavities from the lingual aspects of the central, lateral and cuspid teeth, all of which were found to contain dead pulps. Then a splint which we had made of vulcanite was placed in the mouth, and to this the central, lateral and cuspid were securely ligated. This was to prevent the dropping out of these teeth during the operation, which would otherwise undoubtedly have occurred. I then made a linear incision about an inch and a half in length, parallel with the margin of the gum, and about one-half of an inch above the margin. In then passing down into the gum, the alveolus was found to be entirely dead, some of it absorbed and carried off with the pus, and a number of the dead pieces were lying detached in the wound. These were removed with gouges, chisels and spicula forceps. We found as we went on a considerable portion of the anterior external face of the maxillary bone was involved. When the bone had all been removed, it was found that we had a space presenting an aperture about an inch long, and three-fourths of an inch high, and perhaps nearly an inch deep. It extended posteriorly to the antrum, and in front to the median line. The palatal surface or floor of our cavity was all devoid of bone, and naught remained there for quite a space save a mucous membrane partition separating it from the mouth. In one place the cavity opened into the nasal fossa, about an inch back from the nostril. The roots of the lateral and cuspid teeth projected entirely bare of any bony investment into this cavity, as also did the apices and sides of the bicuspid and central. During our operation the cuspid came out entirely, and although we began to think that it was a very forlorn chance to save any or all of the teeth, we tied it back in its place.

Every step in the operation, it should be noticed, was done under constant irrigation with bichloride of mercury solution, and all the probes and instruments were thoroughly immersed in this antiseptic wash before and during use. We now plugged up the opening with iodoform gauze. The next day considerable swelling of the face was found, but otherwise everything seemed favorable.

Upon removing the dressing we found, to our satisfaction, not a trace of pus, but healthy lymph, and every evidence of a healthy wound. To be brief, I will say that from the day of the operation we saw no pus; about every three days we removed the dressing, we found the reparative process going on splendidly from the bottom; soon the opening into the nares closed, bone formed around all the teeth, and at the end of about six weeks from the time of the operation, osseous tissue had been formed around the roots of all the teeth. The patient's general health began to mend from the time of three or four days after the operation. The next and last case with which I shall burden you is one of very frequent occurrence in our practice; not usually very dangerous to the general health, it is none the less often attended with very considerable loss of alveolar substance and loosening of the teeth. The disease is sometimes very obstinate in yielding to local medication, or to the use of aromatic sulphuric acid, but by simple surgical removal of the diseased bone it will almost always cease. To illustrate, I will select at random from a number of similar cases in my practice.

Case 3. Miss M— applied to me to relieve her of a discharge issuing from a fistulous opening in the gums, between the superior left lateral incisor and cuspid. She reported the discharge to have existed almost continuously for over a year. Upon examination of the lateral, which was filled upon its mesial surface with gold, I easily discovered it to contain a dead pulp. I immediately drilled a hole through the lingual aspect of the tooth, and, upon entering the pulp cavity, found it to be filled with a fluffy substance, which upon removal, was found to be a mass of cotton wool, which the patient said had been placed there about two years ago by a dentist who had filled the tooth. I then, after as thoroughly cleansing the pulp canal as possible, filled the said canal with a dressing of floss silk and iodoform, and dismissed my patient for a week. When next she came I removed the iodoform dressing, thoroughly washed out the canal, and entirely filled it with oxychloride of zinc. I then took a probe, and passing it down through the fistulous opening was able, easily, to discern the presence of soft, dead bone, which I proceeded to remove with a bur in the dental engine; however, to reduce pain and diminish hœmorrhage, I injected as deeply as I could penetrate with a blunt hypodermic needle into the fistula, about eight minims of a four per cent aqueous solution of hydrochlate of cocaine. I then proceeded in two or three minutes to remove with the bur the dead bone, which

I could easily detect by its feel, and entered a cyst or enclosure, about the size of a small marble, to which the fistula led. The sides of this I thorougly scraped until I was sure the walls were composed entirely of live bone, and also burred off the apex of the root of the lateral incisor which was projecting into the wound. I then very thoroughly washed out the cavity with carbolized water, and after inserting in the orifice of the wound a tent of antiseptic cotton I dismissed the patient, who said she had suffered during the operation no pain. The next day I found some pus, and injecting freely with hydrogen peroxide directed her to use it herself three times a day. She did so ; in three or four days the pus ceased to flow, granulations of new tissues began to appear, and in about four weeks the orifice healed up, and since then has shown no disposition to recur. I would say that I have purposely selected cases from my case-book, occurring and operated upon five, six, and seven years ago, since I have been enabled for years, and up to the present writing, to watch said cases, and can certify that there has been in them no recurrence of disease. The last one, that of the alveolar abscess with cyst, and fistula, is selected at random as a type which is constantly presenting itself in your essayist's practice, and being treated by him substantially in the manner described, yielding in the great majority of instances satisfactory results. In brief, my efforts are directed by every justifiable surgical or mechanical means, in *caries* toward changing a chronic ulcerating condition of the bone, progessive, and non-healing in its character, into a healthy wound, presenting features of acute inflammation and capable under skillful, and judicious treatment of casting out new products, and repairing waste of tissue. I have found it expedient in latter years to abandon the dental engine as a means of burring out carious bone, as I have found by experience I can follow more closely and safely and feel more delicately and surely my way, with a system of gouges, chisels and scoops which I possess. In closing this essay, which your indulgence has permitted me to present, I would mention with thanks the assistance which I have received from works on kindred subjects by Christopher Heath, McNamara, T. Bryant, Holmes and our most worthy confrères Drs. L. C. Ingersoll and G. V. Black.

DISCUSSION.

Dr. W. H. Atkinson of New York, in opening the discussion, said: "I labor under some difficulty as to how to express myself in

justice and truth in portraying the manner in which the reading of that paper has affected my mind. If some one had
read it in a foreign land and said that Atkinson did it, I should
not be surprised, for there are so few points in it that I can deny.
I have never heard an approach to the comprehension, diagnosis
and treatment of such cases so nearly like my own as this presents,
and I can not find fault with anything respecting it, excepting that
it might be considered a little technical.

Just at the close of the delineation of his last case, reference was
made to the reparative process, which he denominated inflammatory—now I deny that the reparative process is ever inflammatory
—that it has ever arisen to the status of deterioration of the
nutrient action of the tissues to be entitled to that word, or else it
has been restored by retrograde metamorphosis and has assumed
the condition of embryonal structure, or what is called granulation
tissue, by men who are scientifically up in this matter, and yet they
do not sufficiently define what they mean by granulation tissue,
either macroscopically or microscopically, for us to understand
them.

As to the manner in which we shall get rid of either carious or
necrosed portions of bone, that should be left to any man as intelligent as the writer of the paper has proved himself to be. We can
not lay down rules by which manipulations shall be made upon the
living economy ; there must be some intelligence and honor in the
individual to enable him to be at liberty on the subject, or he is not
fit to touch the case at all. This bears upon a subject that I have
been interested in for many years, and am now working at it to the
best of my ability, that is, dealing with the subject of retrogression
of the tissues when pus is present. I will not attempt to denomi-
nate the processes through which retrograde metamorphosis, under
the stress of inflammation, passes. When the tissues have been
swollen, congested, and melted down until the granules of the
embryonic structure are separated from each other, remaining with
a few, perhaps, connective tissue cells or protoplasmic strings, or
are entirely separate, that is pus. It is never green ; it is never
offensive ; it is never reparative as far as corpuscles are concerned.
The fluid contained within the abscess cavity or chasm of the de-
teriorated tissue, is capable of generating a rather poor sample of
reproductive tissue. When retrograde action shall have gone far
enough to have not only dissolved all the protoplasmic strings in

this reduced tissue, leaving the granules, improperly called leucocytes by writers on this subject—when the metamorphosis, I say,
shall have gone into the melting process, one step before the reparative process you get something worse than dead corpuscles. They
are not entirely dead yet ; they proliferate and segmentate into a
mulberry mass after that, and do not build up the tissues. We get
sanies after this process of retrogression has gone further on, developing a virulence by the so-called chemical action within the
remaining connective tissue involved in the territory, constituting
capillaries, arterioles, venoles, and the white corpuscles of the connective tissue. In these cases the abscess is not only composed
of pus, but of sanies and ichor, a greenish tinge or bluish streaks
being noticeable.

Dr. T. W. Brophy of Chicago: I am very glad that Dr.
Martindale came here and read this paper, for he has very
clearly drawn the line between that which is generally denominated alveolar abscess, and that which is termed caries (although
incipient) of the maxillary bone. He has gone still further ;
he has discussed the subject of necrosis, simply the death of bone
a little different in form. If I have ever felt the pulse of the
dental profession and ascertained the condition of it in this respect,
I feel that I have learned that there is not that importance given
to this subject of incipient maxillary caries that there should
be. We find oftentimes that cases coming into our hands which
have been treated months and months for the cure of alveolar
abscess without success, are simply cases of caries where the bone
is in process of disintegration, and which will not be restored to a
normal condition without resorting to different procedures. For
example, the last case cited by the doctor where the septum had
been destroyed by a slow process of disease, and where the next
teeth as well as the entire surface had lost the bony structure in the
beginning. Probably in this case he had a simple fistula, which
continued to increase in size until the gum-tissue sloughed away
and beneath it was the diseased bone.

While I do not desire to enter into a discussion of the pathology
of caries and necrosis of the maxillary bones, I want to state to you
some of the methods that I adopt in the treatment of these cases.
I will speak first of caries, which is an ulceration of bone or molecular
destruction. We have here, for example, a territory of softened
bone at the apex of a tooth, the pulp of which is dead, and which

has its origin from an alveolar abscess; the usual treatment of that abscess is to open into the tooth, make applications, if it is not a fistula, and expect nature to effect a cure. It does not do it, and why? Because the disease has gone beyond the tooth ; it is a disease of the territory beyond, so we resort to some surgical methods for the purpose of effecting a cure. What are these? The method that has been delineated by Dr. Martindale, and indorsed by Dr. Atkinson, and which I believe was first introduced by Dr. Pollock of St. Bartholomew's Hospital of London, has already been explained. But this method of procedure is sometimes not sufficiently rapid. We are not able to control our patients for a sufficient length of time to effect a cure by it, consequently we must resort to surgical interference, and that has been described. What I have to say in reference to that, is simply a little in addition to what has been said. I indorse the methods that have been described by Dr. Martindale. I want to make this statement: he says he has discarded the surgical engine ; I have not. In a case where the caries is not very extensive I would make an incision, expose the diseased parts, and, if need be, I would at once pack them with iodoform gauze, or what I think is better the boracic acid gauze, thus getting its antiseptic effect and obviating the disagreeable odor that comes from iodoform. Pack it and dismiss the patient for a day, and on his return remove the packing, make an ocular examination of the parts so as to see exactly what we have, to see how far the disease has gone, whether it has involved several roots or one root of the tooth, then we know how far to proceed intelligently with our operations. It is true the sense of touch may enable us to determine whether the bone is softened ; we may without the aid of vision be able to make the proper surgical operation, and not go beyond the territory involved by the disease. The former method of procedure is better. We take a long sharp bur, passing it into the osseous cavity, excising the ends of the roots of the tooth. Why should we cut these off? Simply because they stand up there and do not serve any useful purpose, and are often a source of irritation ; they interfere with the formation of new tissue, consequently it will be far better to dispose of them. Having done this, we cleanse the cavity, and pack it as before directed. I prefer the crystals of boracic acid in these cavities, because they dissove more slowly than pulverized acid ; they are more constant in their action — in other words, we retain the antiseptic agent longer by using these crystals

which dissolve more slowly than any other agent. ·Having packed
the wound with some antiseptic gauze, a few days later we make
another ocular examination, and if we see little red eyes (granulations) shooting up here and there over the surface of the part, it will
soon be well, for we know that that is an effort on the part of nature
to close the cavity and effect a cure. Then what I deem far better
than any fabric for the closure of the wound or part is wax, which
may be softened and moulded to the cavity ; remove the excess
upon the surface, and then replace. Why do we do this? Because
a wax plug is better than a fabric plug for the reason that it
is not capable of absorbing moisture, and it is more cleanly.
It doesn't take up any secretions and excite further irritation. We may from time to time remove the inner surface of the
plug, relieve it after a little time, so that granulation may go on;
then by and by the cavity will he filled to an extent which will prevent the retention of the plug longer. This plug must be kept there
so as to prevent closure of the wound. If the orifice of the wound
closes, the secretions will be retained within the cavity, and trouble
will ensue.

A word about the extreme cases, where necrosis has occurred
and the roots of soft teeth have become exposed—in short, where
the entire alveolar processes have been destroyed and the teeth
retained. Our friend, Dr. Atkinson, says he would not have believed that years ago. I have had a number of cases where all the
alveolar process was gone, and by careful retention of the teeth by
splints held them there and secured a new formation, which was
sufficiently strong to retain the teeth in place and make them serve
the purpose for which they were made.

FEBRUARY 6TH—SECOND DAY—AFTERNOON SESSION.

The Society was called to order by the President, promptly at
3 P. M.

ANTISEPTICS.*

By G. V. BLACK, M.D., D.D.S., CHICAGO, ILL.

It will be the object of this paper to give in some detail the results of experiments undertaken for the determination of the value
of the essential oils as antiseptics. In the progress of the experimentation, however, it was found desirable to include a number of

---

* The experiments reported in this paper were begun under the auspices of
the Odontological Society of Chicago.

the more popular antiseptics by way of comparison, and these will be reported with the others, both for the information they give and for the better understanding of the relative value of the limited number of essential oils thus far studied. But in addition I shall devote some time to the consideration of the forms and modes of the use of antiseptics.

For some years past the use of the essential oils as antiseptics has been gaining favor. But in looking up the literature of the subject I have been impressed with the lack of exact knowledge of their value. It is a fact worthy of notice that some of the reputed antiseptics in use are not such as should be relied upon in surgical procedures, nor in the treatment of suppurative affections. The most notable case is that of iodoform, which has been so widely used as to form one of the supposed necessaries of the surgeon's case, and is yet without antiseptic value. Although this has been repeatedly pointed out, both by expert clinical observers and by experimentalists, I am sorry to say that it is still widely used for this purpose. Whatever may be the therapeutic value of iodoform, it is certain that in any solution that can be made in water or broth, it is in no sense an antiseptic and should not be used with this end in view. It is with the hope that it may in some measure serve for the prevention of such mistakes in the future that these experiments have been undertaken.

In doing such a mass of experimentation as I have now to offer you in the time I have been able to catch of evenings after busy days, I would be fortunate indeed if I should be found by those who may follow me, to have been entirely free from error, though I have made every effort at correctness. I have carefully repeated the observations upon those substances that have seemed useful for the purpose of eliminating all sources of mistake.

I wish to be understood as to the use of the word antiseptic. We are so unfortunate as to use, in connection with the therapy of micro-organisms, some words in a very loose way. Such is the case with the words antiseptic and disinfectant. Now, in my use of the word antiseptic I wish it distinctly understood that I do not mean disinfectant. An antiseptic is a drug that *inhibits the growth* of microbes. A disinfectant is a drug that *destroys* microbes. The same drug may be both antiseptic and disinfectant, but for these different purposes they would be used differently and in different proportions. As a general rule we are unable to use disinfectants,

as such, in medicine and surgery, for the reason that the very poisonous properties of such medicaments would do more harm than
their disinfectant property would do good. Dentists may use such
in the roots of teeth with good effect, and in some favorable positions they may be used in contact with the soft tissues, as in very
small abscesses. But for the most part we must be content with the
milder remedies, and rely still more on aseptic procedures.

In the study of the essential oils very great difficulties have
been encountered. In the first place the quality of the individual
oils is uncertain. These are compound bodies that are probably
liable to fluctuation in quality, dependent on the condition of the
plant used, even when carefully prepared. Furthermore, the conditions of their production are such, with a large number of the
oils, that the preparation must be undertaken where the plant
grows, by persons of no scientific knowledge of the subject. This
being the case, it often happens that the most desirable parts of the
plant are mixed with undesirable parts, or even parts that injure
the product seriously. For instance, the leaves of a certain tree
yield a certain oil, and the bark another oil of different quality.
Now, if the person distilling the oil throws in twigs with the leaves,
the oils will be mixed and uncertain in quality. Besides this, there
is much perplexity arising from their adulteration. Taking these
facts into consideration, I can say no more than that the specimens
of the oils that I have had, have yielded such and such results. The
same oil in name may be different in the next specimen. I think,
however, that it may be stated that, as a certain drug becomes
valued in a pure state, tradesmen will readily be found who will furnish
it in that condition. In the uses to which the essential oils have been
put in the past, strict purity has not been of serious consequence.

Mode used in testing the antiseptic value of the oils.—The modes
I have used in the exeriments which I will report are of consequence to any one who may wish to test the correctness of my
findings. Furthermore, it is of consequence that these be closely
scanned by the profession as to the correctness of the procedures
by which the results have been attained. I will, therefore, give
them very briefly, but in sufficient detail to enable persons of
reasonable skill in this kind of experimentation to follow me, or
judge of the value of my findings.

In all of my work an incubating oven with a well-adjusted ther-
mostat for the automatic regulation of the temperature has been

used. The temperature was kept at ninety-nine degrees Fahr. I have used beef broth peptonized and sweetened, and then carefully neutralized. Much care has been used that this should be even in quality in all of the experiments, so that the proportional representation of the values of the different medicaments should not be seriously marred by variations in the sustaining power of the culture medium. This is one point that has, I fear, not received sufficient attention from some who have tried this class of experimentation; and indeed it is a point of no little difficulty. The infection of the broth has always been made with my own saliva direct, under as near analogous conditions as possible; thus avoiding the use of micro-organisms that may have been weakened in vigor by cultivation under artificial conditions. They have therefore been with mixed growths which gives more severe tests than isolated varieties. The tubes used have been graduated to insure certainty in measurements of the broth, while very finely graduated pipettes have been used for the addition of the medicaments. In all cases control tubes have been used as a guide to the value of the plant. Each observation has extended over a period of five days, unless growth of microbes has been demonstrated earlier. And, what is no less important, notes of everything deemed of value have been written when observed. Nothing has been left to the memory. In some classes of experiments notes have been made each twelve hours, in the others each twenty-four hours. It has been my aim to so thoroughly systematize the work as to make the conditions of each of the experiments equal, as nearly as possible, except where these conditions were purposely changed, and noted. The metric system has been used for convenience in calculating proportions, but all of my statements are made in the form of one part of the medicament or solution added to so many parts of the broth. It will be noted that this does not represent percentages. In the construction of tables of results, I have in each case copied actual experiments, as the notes were made at the time, but of course do not give all of the experiments with each drug, only a representative one selected from those made.

Relating to the essential oils I have made the experiments in two classes, the one with the oil in substance and the other with the aqueous solution of the oil. Since the solubility of the oils is not accurately known, the quantitative value of the solution becomes much more important than the quantitative value of the oil in substance, for the reason that in most of the uses of antiseptics it is only the solution that is effective. This is not so generally true of the oils as of crystalline substances; for in many cases the oil in substance may be effective, but crystalline substances can not act at all until dissolved. For this reason I have in all cases given the quantitative value of the solutions of crystalline substances.

It seems to have become a custom among experimenters in this field to state effective proportions in the greatest number of figures possible; or to give the proportions of drugs in substance no matter how insoluble they may be, or in what proportion the solution may be effective. This is liable to be very misleading for the reason that it gives no idea of the range of value the drug may possess. This *range of value* is found in the difference between the saturated solution and the greatest dilution that will inhibit growth. For instance, if a given drug is effective as an antiseptic in a tube test in the proportion of 1 to 1100, and dissolves only in the proportion of 1 to 1000, it has a very short *range* of antiseptic value and must fall below the line of effective work the moment it is mixed with the secretions of a wound. On the other hand, if a drug dissolves in the proportion of 1 to 1000, and is effective in the proportion of 1 to 10000, (1 to 10 of the solution) it has a fairly long range of value; and in this case the saturated solution may be much diluted by the secretions and still do effective work. With very poisonous drugs that are freely soluble, this range must be supposed to begin with such a dilution as may be borne by the tissues without serious evil effects. I should not say that such a drug as the first named could be of no real value, but it is evident that its use should be limited to a class of cases in which it would not be mixed with secretions or other substances calculated to limit its action, or cause it to fall below the line of active work by reason of dilution. I have therefore thought it well to give the value of the solutions as such, and in this way illustrate the range of value of the drugs studied. With those drugs that are too poisonous to be used in saturated solution, the degree of concentration that may be borne will vary so much in different cases that no statement can be made. I think that a study of the tables presented will demonstrate the usefulness of this form of presentation.

All solutions are saturated aqueous solutions, except those in which the percentage is given. The solutions of the essential oils are all made in the following manner: An excess of the oil is mixed with water by violent shaking continued for some minutes. It is then placed in the incubating oven, where the temperature is 99° Fahr., for twelve hours. It is then again violently shaken and returned to the oven for another twelve hours, twenty-four hours in all. It is then carefully filtered, and if not perfectly clear and free from all appearance of oil it is refiltered until it is clear. This filtrate is then used as the solution of the oil. The same plan has been used in making saturated solutions of the crystalline substances.

In all of the tables, the numbers that proved effective in the prevention of growth are printed in ordinary type, while those that were found ineffective are printed in boldface type. If growth has not occurred within the first twenty-four hours, but has occurred within the second, a star follows the number; and if growth has been delayed until the third day, or could not be demonstrated until that time, two stars will be found, and so on.

I have also grouped the derivatives of the oils with the oils to which they belong, otherwise I have placed the medicaments in the table alphabetically:

TABLE.

Aseptol,(Merck's 33.3% sol.). 1–10, 1–15, 1–20, **1–25**.

Benzoic acid, (sol.)........1–1, **1–2**, **1–3**.

Beta-naphthol, (sol.)......1–1, 1–2, 1–3, **1–4**, **1–5**.

Boracic acid, (sol.)........1–4, 1–6, **1–8***, **1–10**.

Carbolic acid,...........1–300, **1–560**, **1–900**.

    5% solution............1–8, 1–10, 1–12, 1–15, **1–20**.

Copper sulphate. (sol.).....1–100, **1–200***, **1–400**.

Creosote, (commercial)....1–400, **1–500**, **1–900**.

    Morson's wood tar,......1–700, 1–910, **1–1200**.

    Solution............1–1, 1–2, **1–4**, **1–8**.

Hydronaphthol, (sol.)......1–1, 1–2, 1–3, **1–4**, **1–5**.

Iodoform...............Growth in saturated solution among the undissolved powder.

Bichloride of Mercury.....1–25000, 1–50000, **1–100000**.

    1–500 solution..........1–50, 1–100, **1–200**.

Resorcin (6.5% sol.)........1–4, 1–6, **1–8***, **1–10**.

Oil of bergamot.........1–200, **1–400**, **1–720**.

    Solution..............**1–1**, **1–4**, **1–5**.

Oil of cajeput............Growth in the emulsion.
Oil of cassia.............1–3000, 1–4000, 1–5000*.
Solution..............1–2, 1–3, 1–4, 1–8, 1–10*.
Oil of cinnamon (Ceylon)..1–2000, 1–2700*, 1–4000.
Solution...............1–1, 1–2, 1–3, 1–4*, 1–5.
Oil of cloves.............1–1100, 1–1200, 1–2000.
Solution..... ....1–1, 1–2, 1–3*, 1–4.
Eugenol.................1–640, 1–800, 1–1200.
Solution..............1–1, 1–2, 1–3, 1–4*, 1–5.
Oil of copaiba...........Growth in the emulsion.
Oil of coriander ....Growth in the emulsion.
Oil of cubebs............Growth in the emulsion.
Oil of eucalyptus.........Growth in the emulsion.
Eucalypti extract,......1–100, 1–240, 1–480.
Solution ....1–1*, 1–2, 1–3, 1–4, 1–5.
Eucalyptol............1–100, 1–380, 1–650.
Solution............1–1, 1–2, 1–3, 1–4, 1–5.
Oil of fennel.............Growth in the emulsion.
Oil of mustard ....1–1000, 1–1500, 1–2000.
Solution ....1–1, 1–2, 1–4*, 1–6, 1–10.
Oil of pennyroyal........1–480, 1–720, 1–960.
Solution ....1–1, 1–2, 1–3, 1–4, 1–5.
Oil of peppermint........1–375, 1–600, 1–800.
Solution ....1–1, 1–2, 1–3, 1–4, 1–5.
Menthol, (sol.) ....1–1, 1–2, 1–3, 1–4, 1–5.
Oil of Sassafras..........1–270, 1–540, 1–800.
Solution ....1–1, 1–2, 1–3, 1–4, 1–5.
Oil of thyme ....Growth in the emulsion.
Oil of turpentine, (Merck's
rec.)................1–500, 1–600, 1–800.
Solution ....1–1, 1–2*, 1–3, 1–4, 1–5.
Terebene ....1–480*, 1–800, 1–1400.
Solution ....1–1*, 1–2, 1–3, 1–4, 1–5.
Terpinol..............1–520, 1–720, 1–960.
Solution ....1–1, 1–2, 1–3, 1–4, 1–5.
Oil of valerian..........Growth in the emulsion.
Oil of wintergreen ....Growth in the emulsion.
Salicylic acid, (sol.) ....1–1, 1–2, 1–3*, 1–4, 1–5.
Oil of wormseed.........1–280, 1–720, 1–880.
Solution ....1–1, 1–2, 1–3, 1–4, 1–5.

EXPERIMENTAL TESTS IN BROTH CONTAINING FIVE PER CENT OF EGG
ALBUMEN.

In the following tests three solutions of the bichloride of mercury were used. A 1–500 solution of bichloride of mercury was made and divided into three equal parts. That marked (p) was left plain. That marked (a) received 5 per cent of hydrochloric acid. That marked (s) received 10 per cent of chloride of sodium.

Solution (p), 1–5000, 1–7500, 1–10000, 1–15000.

Solution (s), 1,5000*, 1–7500*, 1–10000, 1–15000.

Solution (a), 1–5000*–, 5–7500*, 1–10000, 1–15000.

Solution (p), 1–1000, 1–2000**, 1–3000**, 1–4000*.

Solution (s), 1–1000, 1–2000***, 1–3000**, 1–4000*.

Solution (a), 1–1000, 1–2000. 1–3000, 1–4000.

Carbolic acid, (5 per ct. sol.).1–8, 1–10, 1–12, 1–15, 1–20.

Oil of cassia, (sol.)........1–3, 1–5, 1–8, 1–10*.

Copper sulphate (sol.).....1–100, 1–200, 1–400.

A perusal of the table will show that, of the oils thus far studied, some are of no value, while there is a wide difference in the range of antiseptic value of those that inhibit growth. Some of those of widely reputed merit are shown to be of no value whatever. This is especially true of oil of wintergreen, of which salicylic acid is a derivative. I tried a number of specimens of this oil obtained from different sources, and microbes grew freely in the emulsion of each, while salicylic acid has a moderate range of antiseptic value. It is to this matter of *range of antiseptic value* that I wish especially to call the attention of the profession at this time. I think that very few appreciate the shortness of the range through which any drug may be used for this purpose. That is to say, the point of concentration that will inhibit the growth of microbes is generally not very far from the point that will seriously injure any animal tissue to which it may be applied, or be liable to produce toxic effects by absorption; or, if the medicine is one that is but feebly poisonous to the animal tissues, its range of antiseptic value is very short indeed. There are but few and uncertain exceptions to this rule among the antiseptics that I have thus far studied. The general rule is: the greater the range of antiseptic value, the more dangerously poisonous the drug. Bichloride of mercury has a very great range of antiseptic power, in the absence of albumen, and it is also very poisonous. On the other hand, the preparations of eucalyptus are very feeble poisons, so feeble that they may be used upon the tissues almost at will. But at the same time my trials show them to be very feeble antiseptics, and to have a very short range of value indeed. Nothing less than the saturated solution is effective in inhibiting growth. The specimens of the oil that I have had have not been effective in any proportion, but the other two preparations, eucalypti extract and eucalyptol, have been so, and these really exert a restraining power that I am unable to express in my tables. Indeed, I do not feel that I yet understand this power which I find so prominent in eucalypti extract, and especially in oil of cassia. For instance, microbes grow promptly in a broth to which an equal volume of the saturated solution of the eucalypti extract is added, but the growth seems abnormal to such a degree that the specimen has no resemblance to the control tube. The broth usually remains entirely clear, while waxy bulbs grow up in the bottom of the tube, or cling to its sides. This character is presented, lessening in degree very slowly as the dilution is increased, so that in one of the solution to four of broth the growth is usually less than one-fourth that in the control tube, and has a very different appearance. It is in this restriction of the growth of microbes that this drug has its value, rather than by its complete inhibition of growth.

This peculiarity is still more strongly expressed in the oil of cassia, and in this case it is united with a fairly wide range of antiseptic value. Indeed this drug presents the widest range of power, all things considered, of any that I have thus far studied. That is, if we consider its use in substance, in the emulsion, in solution, and in relation to its behavior toward albumen, which will be especially considered presently. The drugs most likely to dispute this are carbolic acid, boracic acid, and possibly resorcin and aseptol. Its virtues, as is the case with all of the powerful antiseptics, receives a check in the development of its irritating properties. This is sufficient to blister the skin after rubbing on the oil three or four times a day for two days. I have used it in this way in the treatment of some skin affections supposed to be microbic in their etiology, with very prompt results. When the blisters were healed the case was well in each instance. It has also proven the most effective antipyogenic that I have yet employed. It may be used in the form of an emulsion in any but very large abcesses or infected wounds. At my suggestion, Dr. David Prince has been using it in capital surgical procedures with the most excellent results in the prevention

of pus formation and sepsis, but he finds that where the pure oil comes
in contact with the skin and remains for some time it produces a
blister. In dentistry, the pure oil or the oil diluted with a bland oil
makes a most excellent dressing for foul root canals and abscesses.
In substance it should not be frequently repeated in the treatment
of abscesses, however, on account of its irritating property. It is
this oil that renders the 1-2-3 mixture so efficient.

℞ Carbolic acid, (melted crystals)............... 1 part.
 Oil of cassia,................................ 2 parts.
 Oil of wintergreeen,......................... 3 parts.
Mix the oils and add the melted crystals of carbolic acid.

My original thought in the mixing of this preparation was to get the
best possible antiseptic effect of the carbolic acid and at the same
time overcome its evil effects on the tissues by the stimulating effects
of the oils; but I had not used it long until I found that I had something else, something that I never understood fully until I had made
experimental studies of the oil of cassia. Really, the 1-2-3 mixture
has a range of antispeptic value much greater than carbolic acid
without its evil effects on the tissues ; or at least, with a very great
moderation of them.

Two other points in regard to the oil of cassia should receive
mention ; the fluctuation in quality and the deterioration of the
saturated solution by standing. As to the first, I have had a number of samples bought in the market and the results with the best
and worst will suffice.

The saturated solution of the best gave :

1-1, 1-3, 1-5. 1-8, **1-10***.

Of the worst :

1-1, 1-2, 1-3, 1-4, **1-5***.

A difference of considerable moment. Nevertheless, dealers
inform me that the oil of cassia, being one of the cheaper oils,
is much less liable to adulteration than the more costly ones.
But little seems to be known of the production of this oil. It all
comes from the interior of China, and no one seems to know much
about it.

As to the deterioration of the solution, I have but one observation. A bottle of the filtered solution stood in the case at the college from May to January, fully exposed to the light. The following trials were made with it :

1-1, 1-2, **1-3***, **1-4**, **1-5**.

The bottle, unfortunately, had lost its special mark, and I would not risk saying to which of my samples it belonged ; but in any case it shows a considerable reduction of antiseptic value.

I can not now take time for the discussion of special drugs, or even mention many of the articles included in the tables. It will be seen that many of the oils studied are of no value, while some of them may be made useful. A study of the tables in connection with the properties of the oils already well known in our literature, will be a sufficient guide in their use, and the selection of them for special purposes.

Forms of antiseptics for use: In regard to the use of antiseptics in different cases and for different purposes, I should divide them into three forms, each of which has especial advantages.

These forms are : the solution in water, the oil, and the powder.

The solution in water is especially useful for cleaning infected surfaces of wounds, washing abscesses and, indeed, in any case where there is something that can be removed by washing. In the performance of this act the antiseptic is diffused to all parts of the wound or abscess mechanically, to the best advantage. It is more likely to reach every part in this form than in any other ; and this is an advantage that can hardly be over-estimated ; for it is very difficult to reach all parts of an abscess by any mode of procedure now known to us on account of the very tardy diffusion of liquids. And in case the liquid containing the antiseptic in solution does diffuse, its very diffusion and mixture with the surrounding fluids soon dilutes it below its range of antiseptic value. It is therefore necessary that the washing be continuous to obtain the continuous effect of the drug. This is generally impracticable, and for this reason the watery form of antiseptics is very much limited in usefulness. The continuous drip, or the application as often as every fifteen or twenty minutes gives effective results in some favored localities ; but it is very difficult to carry out and occasions much trouble. The continuous bath is still more limited in its range of application. Neither of these can be used in dental practice. With us the watery form of antiseptics should be limited to the cleaning of infected parts. They can not be trusted to prevent septic action for any length of time, for the reason that they so soon become diluted below their range of antiseptic value by mixture with the secretions, or the juices of the flesh. Since studying the powers of antiseptics and disinfectants more closely, my feeling is that it will not do for us to expect to do much disinfectant work in connection with the soft tissues, except in cases in which some tissue destruction can be borne ; and that antiseptics only retard the growth of microbes during their presence in effective. proportions ; hence the necessity for continuous or oft-repeated application. In using these for the purpose of cleaning, much aid may be had by making use of the solution in peroxide of hydrogen instead of water, so as to obtain the mechanical effect of the ebullition of the oxygen evolved in mixing the antiseptic with the secretions. There is possibly some antiseptic virtue in the oxygen itself as well, but I am apt to think that its principal use is the mechanical one. And that is a very important use.

Thorough cleaning is excellent antiseptic work, and the peroxide of hydrogen will do this in many positions where nothing else will, and at the same time carry the antiseptic proper to the more remote parts of the wound or abscess.

THE OILS.

After thorough cleaning with the watery form of the antiseptic we need something that will be more enduring in its effects, and according to conditions should choose between the oils and the powders. If it is an abscess with which we have to deal, an oil which is in itself an antiseptic, or an oil holding the antiseptic drug in solution in effective proportions, may be introduced into the cavity and so agitated as best to bring it in contact with all of its parts. This will, on account of its sparing solubility, remain in position very much longer than the watery forms, and the essential oils are very much more diffusible than the fixed oils, or, indeed any other of the simple forms of the antiseptics with which I am yet acquainted. At the same time a sufficient amount for very extended work is contained in small compass. These are of especial value in such positions as the roots of teeth. In this position any but the most irritating of the antiseptic essential oils may be used to good advantage, and may be relied upon for many days together. In the choice of the essential oils it is by no means necessary that the most powerful of them be selected. It should be remembered in making the choice that the more powerful antiseptics are the more irritating, as a rule. It is therefore often best to choose antiseptics of very moderate range, especially where it is only required to preserve a condition of asepsis. For instance, when a very foul root canal is opened such an antiseptic as the oil of cassia is indicated. After appropriate cleaning, and especially in case cleaning is to be deferred for fear of forcing poisonous material thorough the apical foremen, it may be used in full strength; in which form it may be relied upon as a disinfectant as well. But afterward, when it is only a matter of holding an aseptic condition during the healing of the parts, an antiseptic of shorter range, that is not so liable to injure the tissues, is to be preferred. For this purpose the eucalypti extract in substance is a very useful agent. Its range of actual inhibition is very short, but its injurious effects on the tissues are also very slight, so that the healing process may go on in its presence without hindrance. Furthermore, this oil has a very extended range of restraining influence beyond its range of actual inhibition that is undoubtedly of much use. This oil may be exchanged for terpinol where a little more stimulating effect is regarded as beneficial. The oil of cloves and the oil of cinnamon seem to occupy a middle ground and may be made useful in a large class of cases if the others are in any wise distasteful to the dentist or his patient. The oil of mustard, though a good antiseptic of short range, has an irritant action that limits its use. Yet in cases where it is desirable to arouse the tissues from a state of inactivity this action, in a high degree, is combined with the antiseptic property. It is also one of the most diffusible of the antiseptic oils thus far studied.

Any of these oils may be used in the emulsion if for any reason it is not thought well to use the oil in substance. This form is especially recommended for surfaces of suppurating wounds and the washing of abscesses. In this way small quantities of the oil may be widely diffused and left in a multitude of minute globules to gradually dissolve where it is most wanted, forming a kind of connecting link between the true solutions and the oils in substance. For this purpose a little of the oil selected may be diffused through water by severe shaking, or better, by repeatedly filling and violently emptying the syringe. The milky emulsion thus formed may be used in the same manner as the solution.

I have said that all antiseptics are poisons. I wish to emphasize this statement. They are antiseptic by virtue of their power of restraining life forces ; and their use as antiseptics is permitted only by shades of difference in the action of certain poisons toward the different forms of life, by which they effect the fungi more prominently than the animal tissues.

In the medical sense a drug is not necessarily an antiseptic because it is a poison, for in some cases, as with croton oil and arsenic,
the effect on the animal tissues is the greater, while with others the
effects run almost parallel. Furthermore, each of the antiseptics
has its own peculiar quality of poisonous effect ; and in this respect
a choice is to be made of antiseptics for application in special
cases. For instance, carbolic acid has the property of benumbing
the parts to which it is applied, and the slowing of all the life processes ; the oil of cassia has, on the other hand, the reverse effect of
quickening all of these movements. The one is a depressant irritant, while the other is a stimulant irritant, or excitant. These
properties are happily blended in the 1-2-3 mixture. The range of
value of the eucalypti extract may be increased and its qualities
rendered suitable for this case or that, as they are presented, by the
admixture of the stronger antiseptics, such as five per cent of the
crystals of carbolic acid, or five per cent of oil of cassia, more or
less, as may seem best. In such ways mixtures may be formed
that will unite in the greatest degree such effects as we may wish
to combine with the antiseptic property.

THE POWDERS.

The form of powder has become known in surgery as the dry
antiseptic dressing. For this purpose a crystalline antiseptic in the
form of a powder is required, the saturated solution of which will
not be too irritating. It is sufficiently manifest that very poisonous
drugs cannot be employed for this purpose, for by their solution in
the secretions they would do irreparable injury. As a dry dressing
boracic acid seems to stand at the head of the list. It has a longer
range of antiseptic power than any other that may be used in this
form, and the quality of the irritation produced is not such as to
seriously hinder the growth of granulations, so that wounds heal
readily in its presence. We have, however, in hydronaphthol,
beta-naphthol and salicylic acid, drugs that may be used in the same
way very effectively, though they are of much shorter range of
value, and probably not so diffusible ; and, withal, are not so kindly
borne by the tissues. I once saved a life by stuffing a quinine jar
full of salicylic acid into a stinking gunshot wound at a time when
the patient was in a state of apparent coma from septic fever.

The plan of the dry antiseptic dressing is to heap the powder
in more or less thickness on the wound and apply retaining band-
ages over it so that the antiseptic may slowly dissolve in the secre-

tions and in this way keep up constantly something near a saturated solution in contact with the wound. In this way the dry dressing acts much in the same manner as the oil dressing. Indeed, the object is the same in each case, i. e., to keep an effective solution of the antiseptic in contact with the wound continuously. In this respect these modes of application are the counterpart of the watery forms applied in the form of the continuous drip or the bath, and when applied successfully have the same result with much less difficulty in their application.

This leads me to speak just here of the principle that should hold in the use of all of the antiseptic drugs ; that of continuous application for a long period, or until the wound has healed. The antiseptics are not *disinfectants*. They do not destroy micro-organisms, but only prevent their growth. If the antiseptic is removed, or is reduced below its range of antiseptic value by dilution in the secretions, sepsis may occur. A failure to appreciate this fact is the most general explanation of the failures that are so often seen in surgical practice. How long micro-organisms will live while their growth is held in check by an antiseptic, we do not yet know, but it is certain that they will live for many days in the presence of most of the antiseptics that are safe to use on the tissues. That they die in time there is no doubt, but how long they live is a question not yet solved. They seem to die as a shrub would when placed under conditions that prevent its growth, and are as apt to spring into active life if the conditions of their development are restored by the removal, or dilution of the antiseptic, as the shrub when planted in good soil.

A very serious difficulty in the use of the dry antiseptic dressing in surgery exists in the caking of the powders by being moistened with the secretions, so that, with the reduction of the secretions after a few days, a space is left bewteen this caked material and the surface of the wound. In this case the dissolved antiseptic is soon diluted below its range of antiseptic value and is as completely removed as if taken away altogether. Then, a septic condition may develop under the arch thus formed. If we undertake to prevent this by using but little of the powder, we are liable not to have a sufficient quantity for solution in the secretions and fail to mend matters. In this dilemma it has been proposed by Dr. Prince to make use of the vapor of the essential oils in connection with the dry dressing. This suggestion seems to have sprung from some clinical observations of the excellent effects of the oil of cassia placed in considerable quantity on boracic acid after it was heaped up over the wound after ovariotomy. When this suggestion was communicated to me I at once made a number of experiments with the view of testing its merits, but have found it very difficult to copy the conditions by artificial modes. My experiments were made in this way; a test tube containing ordinary beef broth (about two inches in depth) was infected with saliva, as usual in my experiments, and, before replacing the cotton stopper, a drop of the oil of cassia was placed on its lower end. In this case there was constantly a marked modification of the growth, but not a complete inhibition. A normal growth occurred in the lower portion of the broth while about one-fourth of the upper portion remained clear. These experiments indicate that the vapor of this oil will dissolve in the secretions sufficiently to inhibit growth in the surface portions ; but that its diffusion is not sufficient for it to extend to any considerable depth. From this it seems probable that this kind of combination of an oil with the dry dressing will enhance its value.

Another form in which the crystalline antiseptics have an important, though limited, use is the hypodermic injection. For this purpose, those that are but slightly soluble in water or the juices of the flesh, are dissolved in ether, or similar menstruum, and injected into the tissues. In this case the substance is quickly precipitated in the tissues to be slowly dissolved by the juices of the flesh and maintain an antiseptic action for a considerable time. By this plan some affections may be treated successfully that can not be reached by other forms of application, such as erysipelas, progressive gangrene and those of like nature. This form of application may be occasionally used effectively for the prevention of putrefactive changes in ligated stumps of tumors, such as occur frequently in ovariotomy and other pedicular tumors. The conditions indicating this form of use may be presented about the mouth at any time.

The diffusion of antiseptics, or rather the difficulty of diffusion is a subject that has strongly attracted my attention since I have been experimenting with the drugs named in the tables. In some experiments undertaken for the study of this subject I have found it possible to inhibit growth in the upper portion of the broth in a tube while the lower part was growing in a normal manner. This is very readily done by allowing the solution of bichloride of mercury, in sufficient amount to inhibit growth in the whole of the broth, to run down the side of the tube and spread over the surface of the broth. The tube should be set away quietly. There will be so little diffusion of the bichloride that the broth will be decomposed to within a short distance of the top, while this portion will remain clear and free from growth. Although I have made a considerable number of experiments, I have not studied this subject at all sufficiently, but what I have seen indicates that much may be done to increase the diffusion of antiseptics in the secretions of wounds and the juices of the flesh in the neighborhood of injuries. For instance, A 1-500 solution of bichloride of mercury, in sufficient quantity to inhibit growth in the contents of a certain tube when well mixed, will diffuse so as to inhibit growth but one inch in a horizontal direction. If, however, five per cent of hydrochloric acid is added to the bichloride solution, the diffusion will extend about four inches. The addition of the same amount of common salt will serve to extend the diffusion almost as much. My experiments also confirm what was before known to physicists; that diffusion of liquids takes place very slowly through narrow openings. If two tubes connected by a narrow opening are filled with infected broth and an antiseptic added to one, growth will be inhibited in the one while it will progress normally in the other. There will be little or no diffusion through the narrow opening. These are facts of very considerable importance in the treatment of abscesses and sinuses, and especially infected penetrating wounds; and suggest strongly the value of peroxide of hydrogen as a solvent for the crystalline antiseptics, and the oils as well.

It also shows plainly that we can not expect that the influence of antiseptics laid in root canals will extend to the tissues beyond the apical foramen, unless the medicament is forced through at the time of its application.

The relation of albumen to antiseptic work is of very considerable importance for the reason that its presence contra-indicates one of the most powerful of the antiseptics in use—bichloride of mercury. It has long been known that albumen is an antidote for bichloride of mercury. Yet, on account of its great potency in the absence of albumen, the drug has grown into very extended use in the utmost disregard of the antagonism of the two substances. Experimental tests indicating this have been published by several experimenters, but seem to have been heeded by very few medical men. In order to estimate the degree of antagonism that exists between these two substances, and to see if this applied to other drugs as well, I began a series of comparative experiments, but have not found the time to carry them through with any considerable number of medicaments. I have, however, made fairly thorough work with bichloride of mercury, the results of which are given in the tables. My first ex-periments (not given in the tables) were in reference to the decom-position of the solution of the bichloride when exposed continuously to light. These experiments showed conclusively that for a period of two months, the addition of five per cent of hydrochloric acid to the solution of 1-500 of the bichloride, protected it perfectly ; so that its range of antiseptic value was the same at the end of that time as at the beginning. The plan of experimentation was to mix the solution and set it in the full light of day (not in the sun). This solution was tested for its limit of antiseptic value in a certain broth infected with saliva. Other tubes of the same broth were kept for the purpose, and two tests made each week for the period of two months, without showing any diminution of power. The same solution, without the addition of the acid, lost power very rapidly. ,

The experiments for testing the influence of albumen were first made with two solutions. Each contained one of the bichloride of mercury to 500 of water. To the one five per cent of hydrochloric acid was added, to the other ten per cent of chloride of sodium. The chloride of sodium was added through the suggestion that it would prevent the precipitation of the albumen by the bichloride, which, indeed, seems to be correct. I found that the addition of this solution to broth containing five per cent of albumen, caused no clouding of the liquid, while the addition of the other in even very minute quantities, rendered it milky and if much were added, the albumen was thrown down.

The tests made with these solutions (not given in tables) when compared with the power of the bichloride in the absence of albu-men, show plainly that the two substances are antagonistic ; and that the addition of chloride of sodium is of no substantial advan-tage, notwithstanding the fact that the albumen is not precipitated.

I then made other solutions more carefully, in that a solution of 1 to 500 of the bichloride was divided into three parts in order to be sure that the three were exactly alike, and I give the results with these in the tables. The first was left plain (marked (p) in the tables). The second received five per cent of hydro-chloric acid (marked a), and the third received ten per cent chloride of sodium (marked s).

These solutions were then tried, using for the purpose a new broth, and gave a slightly higher range of value, either from a difference in the broth or in the solutions, it is difficult to tell which. These exper-ments show a great reduction of the range of value of the bichloride in the presence of albumen; and, when we consider that in many of the positions in which the antiseptic is used, there is present from eight to ten per cent of albumen, we can not expect much good from it in a dilution that could safely be placed in contact with the tissues. There is, however, a range of restraint, shown by the fre-quent asterisks in the table, which may account for some benefit in the use of the drug even though it does not fully inhibit growth. It will be noticed that the results with the plain solution are the poorest and the results of the hydrochloric acid solution are much the best. I take it that this effect represents the antiseptic value of the hydrochloric acid rather than any beneficial effects of this agent on the action of the bichloride of mercury.

These results are in substantial agreement with those obtained by Dr. Ernest Laplace, of New Orleans, under the direction of Prof. Koch, of Berlin, he using tartaric acid instead of hydrochloric acid. Also, with those by Van Ermengem, and those by Dr. Bolton, under the direction of Dr. Sternberg and reported by the American Public Health Association, pages 157 to 160 inclusive. The experiments have been very differently made in these different cases and the figures are different; yet the prominence of the loss of power of the bichloride in the presence of albumen is the same in all.

My own clinical observation agrees very well with the experi-mental results. For years past I have used only the 1 to 500 solu-tion, when I have used it at all, as an antiseptic. My reasons for doing so were that it did not seem to effect the purposes intended if used in less strength; and even in that degree of concentration it has not proved a good antipyogenic unless the washing was carried on with a very large amount of the solution.

There can be no reasonable doubt of the effectiveness of the bichloride of mercury in the absence of albumen. Therefore, it ought to hold the place it has gained for the disinfection of instru-ments and of the skin previous to operations. It should, however, be used in greater strength than it is generally employed for these purposes.

I made various tests with the oil of cassia in connection with albumen and all of these gave results that coincide very perfectly with the experiments in broth without the addition of albumen. With this agent the presence of albumen is of no consequence.

The tests of the effects of albumen on the power of carbolic acid show a diminution of its range of value which remained constant, but it is so little that it may be safely ignored in practice.

I have made but few experiments with agents as disinfectants, and these few have been confined to bichloride of mercury and the oil of cassia. I made a number of efforts to sterilize saliva with the bichloride of mercury, all without success. I carried the concentration to 1–250, and planted from this at intervals for two days, with due caution, in well-proven sterile tubes of broth, but every one of them grew freely within the first twenty-four hours. The amount of albumen coagulated in the tubes of saliva shows plainly that the addition of five per cent of albumen to the broth is far too little to give the proper expression to the effect of albumen in the use of this drug in the mouth, in abscesses, or in wounds.

This is in agreement with Dr. Bolton's results (page 159, report of American Public Health Association) in which an addition of 1–100 of the bichloride of mercury was required to effect sterilization of broth in the presence of ten per cent of egg albumen.

Oil of cassia, in full strength, solution or in emulsion, destroys all micro-organisms, in the absence of spores, promptly, but the spores of B. subtilis and some other bacilli resist it for a considerable time. However, my experiments have not yet been sufficiently attested by repetition for me to feel like giving exact figures.

DISCUSSION.

The President then announced that the paper of Dr. Black was open for discussion, and he would call upon Dr. C. M. Bailey of Minneapolis, to make the opening remarks. He said : Mr. President —I have been greatly interested in listening to this paper, and may say I had the pleasure of looking it over yesterday. I feel that the line of argument which Dr. Black has followed in the paper is one of value to us as dental practitioners. Since the day when the germ theory of disease was brought to the notice of the profession, we have had a multitude of agents which have been said to utterly destroy micro-organisms. There is scarcely a magazine, in every issue of which we do not find some one or more of these agents brought

to our notice, said to be perfectly harmless, and capable of destroying the micro-organisms which are the cause of all these diseases.
I notice particularly that Dr. Black's effort in this direction is
to ascertain the value of the different agents, and the range of
their action. He has materially reduced the number of those he
has tried and tested in his test-tubes, many of which we can easily
put to one side. Another thing: I was glad to notice his definition
of the word "antiseptics," for in our teaching, books, and reading
in journals, from which we get our information, I think the word
is used interchangably with the word "disinfectants" and is misleading not only as to the effect of the drugs, but also in our use of
them in practice. Antiseptics may be considered to apply to those
agents which usually inhibit the growth of the organism, and disinfectant to take the place of (but which is not so good a word)
germicide, which seems to be so constantly in use to-day. In this
connection particular attention was called to the fact that these
drugs are used in a strength necessary to destroy the germs which
produce those diseases that become dangerous to the system, making it necessary for us to consider (if these experiments be true)
simply the power of controlling the growth of these microbes until a
cure is effected. And that leads to a consideration of one theory
of the cause of these diseases, which is old, and which I think
should not be lost sight of — namely, that all metamorphosed
tissue results from a lowering of the vitality, either of the general
system or of the part directly attacked. It has been shown that
these microbes have no power of reproduction of growth in the
presence of healthy tissue, that in due course of time if the tissue
is healthy, they will be expelled from the system and a cure affected
without the aid of drugs. An illustration of this perhaps would be
a common boil, where we have suppuration of the dead tissue,
where the system drives out septic matter of itself without the inter-
vention of antiseptics; and, at the same time, we know that the action
of these drugs has not been verified by clinical observations, but
by the experiments of Dr. Black we may find their explanation.
He has called particular attention to iodoform and I think with him
that many times the fact has been established that iodoform does
not destroy the germs nor inhibit their growth. He has spoken of the
oil of cassia. I am not as familiar with the use of that agent as an
antiseptic as I could wish to be, but it maybe we shall obtain some
local stimulus in the use of it.

I will call the attention of the Society to one or two cases bearing upon what I have said. I remember one case that came to me about three years ago; a lady with a central and lateral incisor badly blackened by decay, with a fistulous opening from each of them. They had been under constant treatment for several years. She was very anxious to save them. After cleaning out the roots I found them decayed nearly to the apices. In this case I attempted sterilization of the canal with iodoform dissolved in eucalyptus oil. Both agents you will notice the essayist has shown to be valueless in the matter of inhibition of the microbes. I used the eucalyptus oil to control the odor of the iodoform. After thoroughly disinfecting the canal, or using it for that purpose, I treated it as I always do, by putting a drill through the end of the root, having a clear opening into the sac at the end, then dressed the same antiseptically, with a pledget of cotton pressed to the opening, and discharged the patient for a day or two to see the effects. The next day on making a careful examination of the canal with a probe I found some spiculæ of bone, and I syringed the cavity through the root canal. The canal was so much decayed that I could carry it quite far up, forcing aromatic sulphuric acid at full strength through the canal in both instances. My further treatment was simply with the iodoform and eucalyptus oil, and after two weeks of treatment there was an apparently perfect healing of the parts which have remained healthy to this time.

The other case to which I desire very briefly to refer was that of a gentleman, who had one or two central incisors broken down by decay and desired two gold shell crowns placed upon them. As he insisted upon gold rather than porcelain crowns, I began to prepare the roots and found them infected with signs of abscess. The gentleman left the office and did not return for three or four days. The treatment was the same as in the former case. The root was thoroughly cleansed; I drilled through the end of it into the sac, and syringed with aromatic sulphuric acid until it came out through the gum, and discharged the patient for two days. My further treatment was iodoform and eucalyptus oil, this resulted in a cure in a short time. He has been wearing those crowns for two years, and they are the principal masticating surfaces. I report these simply as clinical cases, which, I am willing to admit, are empirical, in that they do not give to us the method of action of the drug. We simply ascertain by the use of a drug that a certain result is obtained without knowing *why* or *how*, and as such, I must say, that although Dr. Black has shown by his experiments the powerlessness of these agents to destroy the microbes, I think I must still continue to use them.

(Dr. Crouse at this juncture called the attention of the society and the visiting dentists to a circular that had been distributed among them embodying the objects and advantages of the Dental Protective Association.)

. Dr. Sudduth of Philadelphia: The paper which has been read is too valuable to pass without careful consideration, as all of Dr. Black's contributions are. It is one of vital interest to the profession. Many points have been brought out that have been more or less in dispute from time to time, and he has a synthetic method of presenting facts to us that is very valuable indeed. In all our scientific investigations it is absolutely necessary that our results shall be accurate and available, that every means should be taken to avoid error, and I want to call the attention of Dr. Black to one or two points where it seems to me he could have bettered these investigations somewhat, and points we will take up later when he will talk about them himself. This ·work requires a great deal of time, and with the amount of work on hand it is impossible to bring out and complete the report in as accurate a way as is necessary in order to make it thoroughly correct in one paper. I have no doubt he will follow this with other papers in the continuation of his experiments.

I notice that in the use of infecting material he used his own saliva. At different times and under different circumstances that saliva would vary. In other cases it would, to a certain extent, militate against the exactness of the results. It seems to me it would have been better to have used a pure culture under all circumstances. Another point in regard to the use of the words "disinfectant" and "antiseptic". I like his definiton of these terms very much indeed, but the statement was made that it is impossible to ·perform disinfection in soft tissue ; so it is in surgical wounds. The point of interest to dentists in particular is the disinfection of the oral cavity. The oral cavity in a state of health is lined by epithelium and is protected against the action of the medicaments which are poisons, as stated, in their deleterious action upon the tissues. The use of these different agents in the root canals is necessary to accomplish thorough disinfection, and there can be no possible trouble resulting beyond that. Experiments with hydrochloric acid, and with the different acids to prevent the formation of albuminates have been gone over. Dr. La Place, in his work in Berlin, commenced first with hydrochloric acid, and he proved that the addition of this acid with bichloride prevented the formation of albuminates, so that surgical dressings were not only antiseptic but aseptic in their condition ; whereas those dressings that do not have the addition of hydrochloric acid to them, are antiseptic to a certain extent, but not thoroughly so. The formation of a coat of albuminate underneath a dressing permitted suppuration to go on beneath it.

In regard to the use of antiseptics in root canals, there is no antiseptic better than the bichloride or mercury, $^1/_{600}$, with the addition of 5 per cent of tartaric acid, in any condition of the pulp canal where you want an antiseptic which will prevent the formation of albuminates, which has been the objection to carbolic acid in antisepticizing pulp canals. The essential oils in connection with root canals I should not advocate, because the bichloride of mercury, combined with tartaric acid would accomplish the purpose. The use of any oil is objectionable in filling. Where it is possible to use this combination, I should advocate it above all others. Reference was made to the use of iodoform. While it has been proven that iodoform was not a disinfectant, nor in a very high degree antiseptic, yet clinical experience beyond question bears us out in its use, and by the elaboration of iodine we have an antiseptic in this sense. Iodoform to-day is our main reliance, and surgeons are using it constantly in the dry dressing method.

With regard to boracic acid, which has been spoken of in connection with antisepsis, I may say that in ophthalmology, where it has been extensively used, it has been almost entirely discarded, and its place taken by the salicylate and chloride of soda. We want a disinfectant that can be used in pulp canals which will absolutely destroy the microbes found there. The bichloride of mercury disinfects a pulp canal ; the same result may be accomplished by heat. Beyond that we want the same line of antiseptics found in Dr. Black's most admirable combination of 1-2-3. I was sorry he did not give us the results of the experiments with that mixture.

Dr. Thompson of Topeka : I would like to ask whether any of the members have observed that the bichloride of mercury blackens the teeth in cases in which it is used as a canal medicine. The first few cases in which I used it the teeth were as "black as a hat." I do not like to assail a remedy that has so many friends.

Dr. H. A. Smith of Cincinnati : I have listened with pleasure to the presentation of the subject of antiseptics. I have only a word or two to say. I have observed during the last two years that just in proportion as dentists understand this whole subject, are they successful. I have given a good deal of thought to it, and have read almost everything accessible on the subject, although I have made no experiments in the direction which Professor Black has treated us to to-day, but I wish to be understood that this subject is worthy of the closest scientific investigation. If we wish to succeed as practitioners of dentistry it must be through a thorough understanding of the whole subject under consideration.

Dr. Harlan of Chicago: I have not been listening to the discussion, but I have read the paper, and should say, from these carefully conducted experiments, while they seem to and do prove that many of the agents hitherto relied upon as antiseptics are of little or no value—that it opens up for the practitioner of dentistry a newer and pleasanter field, especially as relates to the class of agents that these particular experiments deal with. As many of you know, I have long been of the opinion, empirically, it is true, that in many instances the essential oils possessed properties that were unsuspected, and in fact overlooked ; that while they had held a place in the practice of domestic medicine and dental surgery to a limited extent, yet they were only looked upon as make-shifts and not as possessing real beneficial properties in this direction. Most of you who have given any attention to this subject will remember that it has been stated that at a temperature a little below normal body heat, vaporizable camphors are capable of deposition which are themselves antiseptic. This is the property of the essential oils not considered in the excellent paper of Dr. Black, although in one instance he relates an experiment of placing some sterilized broth in a vessel and moistening the cotton stopper, and the vapor from the oil apparently inhibited the growth on the surface of the broth. That only points in a minor degree to the property I have spoken of as being possessed by the essential oils. At this moment I can not recall to your minds the exact reference where you will find that these camphors are positive substances that have already been recognized by two or three experimental chemists, so it is better to let that pass.

The value of these experiments to oral surgeons and dentists generally can not be overestimated. If you will remember for an instant, in the use of antiseptics in the teeth alone, pulpless teeth particularly, and I might say wholly, that when the dentine of the tooth becomes infected, these oleaginous agents are capable of diffusion to a certain extent through the dentine, but, if not themselves, their vapors will be diffused, and in that way, not being coagulants of tissue, will more thoroughly and completely disinfect the dentine than any of the agents heretofore used for this purpose.

It may be well, just at this point, to say that the definition I have in my mind of atiseptics and disinfectants is not the one conveyed to you by Dr. Black. I would not pretend to try to settle that question here and now, because if the word "antiseptics," as defined by Dr. Black, simply inhibits the growth of the microbe the microbe must necessarily die, so that an antiseptic in that sense would be a disinfectant. It may be seen now that if the microbe is destroyed on account of the contact or presence of the antiseptic, that the object is accomplished just as well as if it were done instantaneously, so that the benefit to the practitioner is the same, and to the patient upon whom he operates.

Dr. J. H. Woolley of Chicago: It is with considerable modesty that I make any remarks before so large an assemblage as this, in the presence of the men who have preceded me, and who have such a grasp of scientific principles that is worthy of any country or clime. Some gentleman, I think, spoke of heat as an antiseptic, and as soon as I heard that, it made me feel as though I wanted to say something upon that subject. I will be brief: I have for three or four years been experimenting with heat in devitalized teeth, and I will give an illustration of a case. I had under my care a blind abscess ; I treated it for quite a long time, using antiseptics. Shortly after I thought that tooth was in a condition to fill although there was considerable trouble there yet. I used medicine thoroughly. I introduced into that root a heated broach, having a continuous heat, enough to vaporize water. After taking the broach out of the pulp canal I discovered a pungent odor, something akin to sulphuretted hydrogen. I worked with that heated broach as much as half an hour, and finally the bad odor ceased. Now, the question I wish to ask is, whether the medicine that was put in that tooth as an antiseptic was effectual? I would like to have that question answered by the scientific men present. I have used heat for three years, and have found it more successful than the other antiseptics.

Dr. G. D. Sitherwood of Bloomington, Illinois : I want to say at the outset that I was greatly interested in this paper, and came to Chicago more to hear it than anything else. There are some few things in it that impressed me very favorably, and one point is this: how to maintain that nicety of equilibrium, or whatever you may call it; notwithstanding that these agents, according to Dr. Black, are poisons, they are the best and quickest antiseptics we have; they are the quickest in action. If we do not use them, what agent or agents shall we use to fully do the work? And if you will allow me, I will say that I have been greatly interested during the last two weeks watching the operations of a physician in Bloomington in treating a case of burn, the patient being a lady whose clothing caught fire and was partially burned, and which is one of those cases in which we do not get much destruction of tissue. How did he cure that case? It was in using antiseptics in such a way that they did not destroy the tissues, but yet inhibited the growth of the pus microbes.

Dr. Black, in closing the discussion, said: Mr. President—In regard to sterilization of teeth or sterilization in the presence of albumen anywhere, I have in my report of the American Board of Health, in which there are a very large number of carefully performed experiments tabulated, together with those by Dr. Bolton, under the direction of Dr. Sternberg, of Washington, showed conclusively the inability to sterilize bouillon to which ten per cent of albumen had been added, with 1-100 of bichloride. Now, it strikes me that we do not want to use this drug in the mouth freely in this strength, and it certainly requires this strength to sterilize the contents of a pulp chamber.

In regard to iodoform, any of you can look these over (referring to his list of experiments.) In the absence of albumen 1-1000 was sufficient to sterilize broth or to sterilize an old culture. In the presence of ten per cent of albumen it is entitled to bichloride of mercury 1-100, which is enough of the bichloride to combine with the albumen and enough remaining to produce a sterilization.

With reference to clinical experience with iodoform, let me say this : it is not a reflection upon the medical profession to say it ; only a few have realized what they should do or are able to do with antiseptics. One of these men a number of years ago said to me,. "Come with me, I am going to make a post-mortem examination on a patient who has just died." It was a case of ovariotomy. Iodoform was used upon the surfaces where adhesion had broken up, and we found the surfaces covered with stinking pus, and the iodoform embedded among it. From that day to this that man has not used iodoform. The fact is, gentlemen, iodoform does not prevent suppuration ; that is its clinical history. On the other hand,. it does seem to have a therapeutic action that is beneficial, but not as an antiseptic.   .

With respect to the 1, 2, 3 mixture, it is very funny. I tried over and over again to reach its limit in the tubes I had ; I could not divide it with the smallest tube I could get. I didn't like to make a solution of it in alcohol and use it in that way. Of course, I did do that with the oil of cassia, and made a 5 per cent solution in order to divide the iodine, and the alcohol would take up the ingredients in the same proportion and we probably would not get a true test. If I had large enough tubes I would have given you the results of this mixture. A single drop in 15 cubic centimetres of broth was always effectual, and that was just as little as I could get.

In regard to bichloride of mercury blackening the teeth, I cannot answer that question I do not know. I have not observed that it blackens the teeth.

In regard to vaporizable camphors, I have not much information on that subject. It is a difficult subject to study. I have not studied the point in relation to the essential oils that Dr. Harlan has referred to. I have noticed that camphors would be deposited upon my tubes; when deposited in sufficient amount I could break it up with the blade of a knife during the making of my solutions.

With reference to heat, which has been spoken of by Dr. Woolley, I would say that there is no doubt but there are good effects from heat, if we can get it where we desire it. We can not get it to all parts of the root canal. It would be a good thing to use in some root canals; it is valuable in some cases, but in others it is not.

Dr. Sudduth referred to using my own saliva for infection, and asked why I did not use the pure culture. I will tell you why. Pure cultures vary at different times more than the saliva of a mouth that is kept in a fairly equable condition. If a man brushes his teeth every day, cleanses his mouth regularly, his mouth will be in good condition, and he will find the same microbes there, and they will be in a healthy state. Microbes in infection are not in a healthy state by any means. In the range of tests made by pure cultures, the figures will run higher than if made by saliva. I have made enough tests to know that saliva is better in conducting these experiments. Another thing I want to say. We are liable to have the foundation pulled out from under us in this work, for certainly the methods employed by Koch and others must fail in time; that is, we must have something better and more reliable. The subject is young yet, and as we increase in our knowledge on this interesting subject we may find flaws in the foundation, where whole blocks will have to be taken out and build in new ones. This is not at all improbable. What I have given you is the best light I have on the subject at present. These experiments were commenced about ten months ago, and the only way we can hope to reach conclusions is by pursuing our investigations in this line.

FEBRUARY 6TH—EVENING SESSION.

The society reassembled at 7:30 P. M., and was called to order by the President.

Dr. R. R. Andrews of Cambridge, Mass., read a paper on "The Development of the Teeth, the Formation of Dentine, and Its Appearance in Health and Decay."

The paper was illustrated by photo-micrographs projected on the screen by means of the oxy-hydrogen lantern. Many of the photographs were made for this demonstration; others were from Dr. W. D. Miller's beautiful specimens of Natural and Artificial Decay.

Dr. Andrews said :

Let me first ask your attention to the consideration of the formation of a tissue that seems to have had but little written about it; perhaps it has been but little understood. I allude to the band of only partially calcified substance which is everywhere found on the border-land of calcification. In studying the formation of dentine with the higher powers of the microscope, from tissues which have become decalcified by the action of weak acids, there is found between what was the fully calcified tissue and the adjacent organic tissue from which it is formed, this peculiar layer, hyaline in its appearance. It has been named Calco-globulin. The sections which I have studied are cross sections of forming teeth on the edge of the calcifying dentine germ. The peculiar globular formations next the formed layer of dentine, show best in tissue that has been in the decalcifying acid for two or three days only. A brief description of the experiments of Prof. Harting and Mr. Rainey, showing the peculiar action of some of the salts of lime, in albumen, may be of interest to us at this point; for they claim by these experiments to have found the clue to the explanation of the development of teeth, bone and shell. Mr. Rainey found that if carbonate of lime be slowly added to a thick solution of albumen, the resultant salt is in the form of globules laminated in structure like tiny onions. These globules, which have been named "calcospherites," when in contact, become agglomerated into a single laminated mass. In the substitution of the globular for the crystalline form in the salts of lime when in contact with albumen, Mr. Rainey claims to find the clue to the explanation of the development of bone, teeth and shells. What he found, was really the first stage in the process of the calcification. Prof. Harting has shown that the albumen left behind after the treatment of these globules with acid, is no longer ordinary albumen. It is profoundly modified, and has become exceedingly resistant to the action of acids, resembling chitine—the substance of which the hard skin of insects consists, rather than any other body. It appears that the lime is held in some sort of chemical combination, for the last traces of lime are retained very obstinately when calco-globulin is submitted to the action of acids, in the same manner as does that layer which is found everywhere on the border land of calcification. In the course of my investigation I have found many sections showing the formation of these peculiar globular masses on the edge of forming dentine or enamel. They are seen next to the dentine, towards the pulp, and apparently among the odontoblasts, even with a low power. The pulp tissue, and the odontoblasts may be pulled away from the layer of dentine, with no appearance of globular masses clinging to it. The dentine edge however, has a glistening appearance, something like the globules mentioned above; and under a high power ($^1/_{12}$ Im. obj.), this glistening edge shows rounded contours, as if there had been globules, which had become in part, the already formed band of dentine. In the substance of some of the odontoblasts, and even in the tissue of the pulp near them, are seen calco-spherites.

The forming layer is at this very early stage of the formation of the dentine, about as wide as the layer of dentine formed, and is also about as wide as the layer of odontoblasts. At a later stage when the calcified layer of dentine is thicker the layer of calco-globulin is much narrower, and I have never been fortunate enough to observe it forming in this manner, although indications of globules and globular masses are never difficult to find within the layer of calco-globulin. In my demonstration on the screen I shall show these globules and globular masses, and where they, by coalescing, are forming a layer.

Let me now call your attention to the subject of dentine in decay, carious dentine. On this subject I wish to say I have very little that is original to offer. Prof. Dr. W. D. Miller, an American dentist in Berlin, has left but little for anyone else to do. His work has been very thorough. He has had the advantage of working beside the foremost mycologist of the age, and his experiments bear the stamp of being more trustworthy and carefully prepared than any of the workers in this special field, either before or since his time. Magitot had made many experiments while investigating this subject, and had produced caries out of the mouth by means of weak acids, that to all appearance, macroscopically, were like natural decay, but here the similarity ceased; for, under the microscope, the appearance presented by the tissue was totally unlike natural decay. Dr. Miller's early work led him to believe, as a result of many experiments, that the first stages of decay were caused by acids, for the most part generated in the mouth by fermentation; and he went to work to determine the nature of this ferment and the conditions essential to its action, to find, examine and describe it. How well he has accomplished his task some of us know. Yet it seems strange that there are so many yet who do not appreciate the importance of this work. I have been most fortunate in having the use of many of Dr. Miller's most valued sections of specimens, both of natural and of his artificially produced decay. These specimens show beautifully the results of his very carefully conducted experiments, and it is the photo-micrographs of these, without any retouching or any change whatever, that I am to show you to-night, where all can see and judge for themselves. As one having had quite an experience in microscopy, I can truly say that it would be impossible for me to tell, under the higher powers of the microscope, which was the section of natural caries or which the section of artificial caries produced by Dr. Miller in one of his pure cultures outside the mouth, either long or cross section. That he was keenly alive to the importance of knowing the cause for the decay of the teeth is shown from extracts of early papers, several years before his more important experiments were made which determined the nature of the fermentation in the mouth, and its relation to dental caries. In 1882 he wrote : " I have for a long time been impressed with the idea that we are all, so to say, afloat in our investigations of dental caries. I look upon the leptothrix buccalis as the chief agent in its production. It produces not alone threads, but bacilli, bacteria, micrococci, and the screw-forms, but I believe it is the coccus form which is the most destructive to tooth tissue. We are reminded that we must keep our eyes open, for there are some things about dental caries of which we have not dreamed." At the end of his article he further says : " If we were able to say with certainty that the leptothrix buccalis generates an acid or an alkali, or that it leaves its substratum neutral, we should be spared a great deal of unnecessary work and thinking."

Possibly the writings of Ficinus, Urdel, Kleuke, Leber and Rottenstein, Wedl, Salter and Milles and Underwood—who had found and described micro-organisms in carious dentine—gave him an inkling into what was really needed to establish the germ theory upon a firmer basis. It is hardly necessary for me to more than outline the experiments made by Dr. Miller, as these investigations are now a part of our history. Those who are not familiar with the extreme care or the great amount of time and labor required to conduct such a series of exact experiments can as yet hardly realize the services that Dr. Miller has rendered to his profession, or how thoroughly he has finished his task. The spirit of the man is shown in this sentence, when he commences the record of his experiments: "If I have been guilty of any oversight, or failed to take all possible precautions to guard against error, I hope that some one will kindly show me where I have gone astray, and put me in the right course again."

His first experiment was to determine whether or not the ptyaline of the saliva could so change starch as to produce an acid. He found that it would not. The starch was changed into sugar, and this was all; the fluid remaining sweet when proper care was taken to prevent the ingress of germs, thus proving that the power of changing to an acid does not belong to the saliva. It must, then, be something else. He took a freshly extracted tooth, removed all food, and saturated the outer portion with 90 per cent solution of carbolic acid to destroy any germs that might be on the surface; then with a sterilized instrument removed a part of the inner portion of the carious dentine. This was quickly conveyed to a sterilized culture medium, composed of sterilized saliva, sugar, starch and water, and then placed in an incubator, together with another test tube of the same culture fluid uninfected. In twenty-four hours the infected culture became acid, while the other did not. Repetitions of this experiment of a sufficient number were made to establish the fact that the acidity was due to the infection. From the cultures that had become acid other cultures were infected which also became acid, showing that Dr. Miller was dealing with an organized ferment, one capable of propagating itself, and a microscopical examination showed that the organisms in the culture were similar to those found in the deeper layers of the decay. In determining the kind of acid produced, Dr. Miller found good use for his special chemical knowledge; his analysis, which was very carefully conducted, proved beyond question that this acid was the common ferment, lactic acid. This acid, newly formed, a waste product of the micro organisms, has a powerful affinity for the lime salts of the dentine. It is constantly being given off, and decalcifies the tissue considerably beyond that occupied by the organisms, thus forming the decalcified zone, free from the organisms, which is everywhere found between the carious and the non-carious dentine. Sugar, that is almost always found present in the mouth, and that changed from starchy food by the action of the ptyaline of the saliva is the natural food for these organisms. There are but two forms found in the deeper layers of carious dentine, one always present, producing lactic acid, the other often present, more than probably producing the same acid, the micro and diplo-cocci. See Fig. 1. They are reproduced in the following manner: A coccus which may be round in the beginning is seen by extension on one axis, to become oval or elongated; soon after it shows a contraction in the middle, resulting in the production of a diplo-coccus, or two cocci, each of which may produce two others in the same manner. The existence of spores has never been detected. Dr. Miller reasoned that if these organisms were the direct cause of caries, he ought to be able to produce true caries by subjecting healthy normal dentine to their action. It is a law with mycologists to determine whether any particular micro-organism is the prime cause of any special disease:

First. That the micro-organism must be found in the blood lymph or diseased tissue of man or animal suffering from, or dead of the disease.

Second. The micro-organism thus obtained must be isolated and cultivated in suitable media, that is, outside the animal body. These pure cultivations must be carried on through successive generations of the organism.

Third. A pure cultivation thus obtained must, when introduced into the body of a healthy animal, susceptible to the disease, produce the disease.

Fourth, (and lastly.) In the tissue of the inoculated animal, the same micro-organisms must again be found. Dr. Miller makes his experiments conform to the same rigid unyielding law, so far as it could be done with the human tooth, and the results are so convincing as to make the truth of this theory self-evident. He procured a decayed tooth and thoroughly sterilized its outer surfaces; then with a sterilized knife-point two portions of the decay were carefully removed from the deepest portion of the caries.   These were carefully placed in two tubes, a piece in each, one containing a fermentable mixture, beef extract, to which 2 per cent of cane sugar had been added, and the other a non-fermentable fluid, beef extract without sugar.   Both of the tubes and their contents had been previously completely sterilized before adding decayed dentine.   He then procured a freshly drawn, healthy bicuspid tooth. This was completely sterilized, and sections made from it, and a number of them placed in each tube.   The tube containing sugar became acid in a few hours; the tube containing no sugar remained neutral.   The sections of the sound tooth that had been sterilized and placed in the first tube with the sugar, soon softened, and at the end of a week could be bent like a piece of soft cartilage.   The sections of the sound tooth placed in the non-fermentable mixture remained unchanged.   At the end of the second week the sections in the fermentable tube became completely decalcified, and could easily be cut with a knife.   Some of these decalcified pieces were placed in a freezing microtome, and thin sections cut, which were stained and mounted in the usual manner.   The stain used was one that stained the organisms and not the dentine.

These sections were then submitted to microscopical examination.   All the appearances found in natural caries were found to be present in those that had been artificially produced.   Compare Figs. 3 and 4.   There were the same distended tubules, crowded full of micro-organisms, breaking down the substance of the dentine.   In some places the walls were broken through, producing oval spaces or caverns in the dentine.   See Fig. 5.   Dr. Miller had thus produced caries artificially by inoculating sound dentine from a culture of organisms found in natural decay, in the presence of the same fermentable substances that are found in the mouth.   In the other tube even the thinnest section did not show a trace of softening.   Could a clearer solution of the problem of deep-seated caries be desired ?   It seems impossible that there can be any doubt in regard to these conclusions.   One better fitted for the work than Dr. Miller it would be difficult to find.   His thorough knowledge of chemistry, of mycology and of microscopy, together with a keen love for investigation, amply meet the highest scientific demands.

In this country there are but a few active investigators in this difficult field of inquiry. There is, nevertheless, a wide-spread interest in their investigations, and a keen desire to know the results. Hitherto these results have been somewhat contradictory; some have uttered opinions entirely opposed one to the other. It has, therefore, been difficult to arrive at definite conclusions. When experiments are so carefully made, and in such a purely scientific manner as they have been by Dr. Miller, we can not fail to attach great weight to his conclusions. He has given the minutest details of all experiments, so that it would be easy for any one of us, if we so desired, to repeat them ourselves. And I feel sure that I speak within bounds when I make to you this statement, that his views are generally accepted by those whose special education in pathology, mycology, chemistry and microscopy best fit them to judge of their reliability. A few extracts from a recent letter of Dr. Miller's may be of interest.

In speaking of some of his recent work he mentions that he has succeeded in making a number of preparations from carious teeth of a horse. He finds the tubules distended, full of micro-organisms, and appear in every way like caries of the human tooth. He also mentions making many from the carious teeth of dogs, These, he says, show the same characteristics. The organisms in the tubules of both horse and dog are chiefly micrococci. In answering the question, have you tried to produce artificial caries by weak acids protecting the tooth, except at the point acted on, he answers : " I have made such experiments as you mention, protecting the tooth with wax, but I have not made many of them. I consider it a useless waste of time. Magitot and others have proven beyond the shadow of a doubt that in this manner the macroscopical appearance of caries can be very exactly imitated. Why trouble ourselves any more about that ? I have, however, a few pieces which, to the naked eye, can not be distinguished from true caries."

He states that the decalcified zone, in advance of the germs, is found everywhere in artificially produced, as well as natural caries, particularly at the sides of cavities in the crown, for the reason that the decalcification extends about as rapidly laterally as toward the pulp. Not so, however, the bacteria. He implies here that they are found only in those tubes opening to the outer surface and exposed to the saliva. See Fig. 6.

At the close of the lecture Dr. Black was called for. He said: I hardly know what I can say to you after such a representation as you all have seen this evening by means of the oxy-hydrogen lantern. It would seem rather more fitting that we all stop and think over it. I had never dreamed of the possibility that it could be made so perfect. You have seen the various micro-organisms and the formation of the tissues displayed on this screen with almost, if not quite, the perfection that we see them with the microscope itself. Only one of us at a time can see these things with the microscope, but here hundreds have been looking at them at once. Then, too, most persons are not able to see them with the microscope, for microscopic observation requires a good deal of training. I have tried in years past to tell something about the subject of micro-organisms with my tube tests before the dentists of Illinois and some other State societies. I have shown them something of the production of acids demonstrated by artificial preparations thrown upon the screen, but here you seem to see things just as clearly. I do not know of any possible deception in these views; they represent simply facts that have taken years to work out. There are many things in microscopy that may deceive us, but certainly we can not be deceived as to the presence of the microbes in the places in which they have been pictured here, for we have seen them with our instruments for several years past.

Dr. Sudduth spoke in the highest terms of the work that had been accomplished by Dr. Andrews. He had dealt with the subject in a masterly manner, and the audience had witnessed what might be reasonably termed a positive demonstration of micrococci as projected on the screen. After seeing these micro-photographs every one had a right to form his opinion as to the function of the organisms. According to his views the matter had been positively demonstrated; it remained with the dentists whether to accept it or not; the literature on the subject was before them.

Dr. L. W. Comstock of Indianapolis, contributed a paper (illustrated by large cartoons) entitled :

ARTISTIC METHODS IN PROSTHETIC DENTISTRY.

Artistic methods in prosthetic dentistry are available to the dentist who has given to the study of the human face a large part of his time and learned what constitutes true proportion; because with this preparation he is enabled at once to see how a plan could be utilized to restore to comeliness a deformed visage.

Although this part of an artist's education is of first importance in esthetic dental prosthesis, I will try to avoid much mention of it;—assume that all here to-night are endowed with the ability to see as an artist sees, and that each one has established in his own mind a standard of proportion and beauty by which the real may be com pared with the ideal, so that I may in proper order present artistic methods.

Fig. 1.

When a patron calls upon me to restore his mouth to a serviceable condition and his face to its normal shape, I provide drawing board, paper, charcoal and pen and then begin an examination of his head and face.

After a general inspection I search for defects and make a record of all that are found, sometimes by writing descriptions of them but more frequently by making sketches.

If the tout-ensemble strikes me, I embody in one sketch (see cut at end of the paper) the result of my observations, but if one position is not sufficient to show all of the features involved in the work of repair a second one is made, so that I have one profile and one full face. Time is wasted in an effort to secure a resemblance, as it is of no practical value in this work. From a position directly in front of the patient and at a distance which will permit me to see the proportions of the entire figure and compare the face with the size of the body, I watch the muscular action of the face, when an animated conversation is being carried on, and make note of any unusual exposure of the teeth and gums.

Fig. 2.

The common classifications of round, square, oval, sharp and flat faces are not explicit enough for the purpose in view, therefore the slight variations from these forms must be seen and remembered. If the face is too long from the nose to the bottom of the chin (Fig. 1) an opportunity is given to the dentist to improve the proportion by making the substitutes shorter than the natural teeth were, but do not lose sight of this fact, that first the discovery must be made that there is a disproportion. The casual observer does not take such matters into consideration when he contracts to construct an artificial denture.

We are obliged to lengthen the face when it is much shortened by the loss of the natural teeth (Fig. 2.) and then it is only a question of how much. The method of dividing the face into

Fig. 3.

three equal parts by drawing lines across the lower part of the fore-head, the end of the nose and the bottom of the chin is universally recognized as the correct course to pursue when representing true proportions. Most of the unsuccessful efforts to restore contour are attributable to ignorance of the laws of art or inability to see the disproportions.

The harmony of the lines in faces must be considered, for in some types they are horizontal, as in the square-faced individual; in the Chinaman they are more or less oblique, and in the features of the plump and beautiful child there are no lines that are not gracefully curved.

Fig. 4.

Truly beautiful forms are always composed of curved lines, and an ornament designed so as to include both curved and straight lines must have two motifs, each one complete in itself. In building up the features these facts must be known and the principles involved must be put into practice.

The least deviation in any part of Hogarth's line of beauty (Fig. 3) mars its symmetry. Make a dent in it, restore it and you have an illustration of a method of facial restoration, for is not the sunken cheek the dent in the graceful curve?

Straight lines have their proper relations one to the other, and I can make some homely illustrations serve me in proving this statement and also to demonstrate the effects of disregarding this fact when constructing dentures.

When the face is broad at the forehead and narrow at the chin (Fig. 4) the two exterior lines are the dominant ones, and all other lines of a perpendicular inclination must harmonize, that is conform; a line through the center leans neither to right nor the left, but the teeth must not all be set perpendicular. The bicuspidati must converge in order to present an acceptable appearance (Fig. 5).

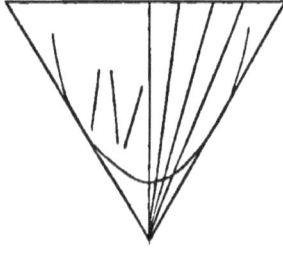

Fig. 5.

Reverse the condition. Look at the man from behind the bar with the narrow forehead and the broad jowl (Fig. 6). The lines diverge as they descend, and pinched in teeth would make him still more repulsive to look upon, but teeth that will stand out like the tail feathers upon a fan-tailed pigeon would suit him well. (Fig. 7).

The application of the principles of artistic adaptation of artificial dentures is in proportion to the deviations from correct form and the construction of gum block teeth is based upon this circumstance. The manufacturers never vary much from the correct proportions, and consequently the placing of the teeth upon the plate can not be wholly wrong, but if it were possible to make them entirely bad some men would do that and then induce people to buy and wear them. A trained eye will readily discern the difference in the size of the sides of the face, that the tip of the nose and the point of the chin are not in line with the center of the mouth; that one side of the upper lip is higher and thinner than the other and that the mouth is too large for the face.

Fig. 6.

When drooping or elevated corners of the mouth are found the line of occlusion of the dentures should be made to conform to the lip line of contact. After these and many other similar points are seen and sketches are made of them, it is better to examine the oral cavity and compare it with the externals before entering upon the study of the profile. When the lips are slightly parted I examine the relative positions of the alveolar ridges to their parting line, and make diagrams like these, Fig. 8 and 9, so that there will be no doubt about either selecting teeth of long or short over-bite or placing them in a position so as to bring about their proper exposure when the mouth is opened. It is often the case that the maxillary ridges are higher on one side than on the other, and while this is the case on the inferior ridge, the superior ridge has a form which is just the reverse; consequently if the denture is built upon these irregularities (Fig. 10) without taking into consideration the lip line of parting, the denture when inserted will have a crooked appearance. But, not satisfied with a superficial examination of the mouth, I seat the patient in the dental chair in a position which will permit me

to look up over the chin into the open mouth, see the shape of the
bones of the face, all at the same time, and compare the size of the
face to the mouth and maxillæ, because neither one alone is suffi-

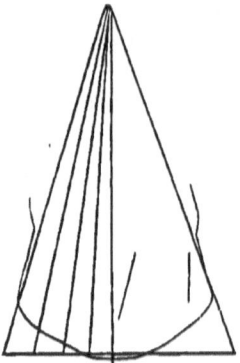

Fig. 7.

cient to determine the size of the arch for the denture.   From this
position depressions in the face that are not common to both sides
are more noticeable and a new idea of their contour is formed, the
defects glare upon me and the patient, who was considered passably
good looking, now appears at a great disadvantage.   Subject your
best girl to such an inspection, and you will find your idol, clay, and
badly modeled.

    The study of the profile is less tedious and the benefits to be
derived from it are more easily seen.   I invariably make the anterior
surfaces of the superior incisors conform to that part of the profile
to which the upper lip belongs (Figs. 11, 12, 13) and take care to
have a reminder of the relation of the lower jaw to the facial line,

Fig. 8.   Fig. 9.

because if the line of occlusion is at an angle of forty degrees to
the facial line and I am not aware of it, the probabilities are that
the denture when inserted in the patient's mouth will deserve the
name of squirrel teeth, because the elevation of the posterior portion of the plate will cause the front teeth to incline inward (Fig. 14).

    It is evident that there can be no truly esthetic prosthetic dental
work, without including an examination of the subject, and we

know that, as a general thing, this examination is at best but superficial.

No two persons see the same thing exactly alike, even from the same standpoint, and but few have the faculty of seeing all that there is to be seen in any object. Trained powers of observation are essential for this work.

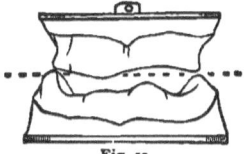

Fig. 10.

The examination completed, the record made, I then sum up the case while all the facts are before me, and *record* the results, so that, with my memoranda, I may at any time take up the work and proceed with confidence.

The impressions taken in the ordinary manner are not satisfactory, and I have made some attempts to improve them. One simple device has given me good results; it is an impression cup, under which is soldered two guides for a bar that has upon one end a half-moon plate, the curved edge of which rises above the rear of the cup, and as far from it as the case demands. Upon this plate wax may be built to fit the roof of the mouth so as to prevent any overflow passing behind, and when the material used for the mould

Fig. 11.

is pressed up into position, the bar may be drawn forward, in order to force the wax or plaster around the necks of the teeth, and thereby secure a correct impression.

I do not overestimate the value of setting casts upon the articulator properly, for it has saved me much time and many failures; therefore I continue to make them very heavy, and then trim them so that they can be fixed at any angle (Fig. 14). It requires no more labor, and if wet paper pulp is used to bank up the impression cup there will be no waste of material. The pulp costs nothing, is bet-

Fig. 12.

ter than wax for this purpose, and when used may be thrown back into a bowl, for use again and again.

When making casts for partial plates, I make sure of flawless plaster teeth by painting the impression with plaster of paris before pouring the mass.

The skill of the carver and the modeler is often needed to bring the cast to proper proportions. Many partial lower dentures are ruined because the cast of the lingual surfaces of the incisors are incorrect. The dentist should know of the line of removal of the impression from the mouth, and when the cast is made, calliper the teeth from the correct side of the cast and carve to proper shape and size. To the uninitiated this may appear to be an unreliable

Fig. 13.

method for securing a well formed cast, but remember that it is a part of the plan adopted by all skilled workmen who re-produce in marble the beautiful forms that have been modeled by the artist-sculptor.

The selection of porcelain teeth is a matter I would be glad to bring up for discussion, but it is too extensive to weave into this paper, and their treatment after selection is but briefly mentioned for the same reason.   I advise grinding, staining, nicking, filling and irregular setting of the so called plain teeth, and sometimes I leave large spaces between them if the age of the patient or other conditions seem to justify such manipulation.

I use a Dr. Land gas furnace to re-bake and re-glaze teeth that have been ground, nicked and stained.   Good results come from the use of china painter's colors—and when a filling is to be inserted it is for the purpose of being seen and I make sure of that.

I would only ring a change upon an often-sung theme if I went into the details of setting teeth so as to meet the requirements of a flat or sharp face, for a straight, thin-lipped mouth, or explain how the expression of the face may be made Satanic by the insertion of dog teeth, but such matters are more suited to the college lecture room.

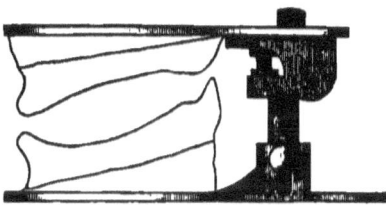

Fig. 14.

In the restoration of the contour of the face the sketches will be found to be of more value than the written notes.   With all these reminders of the conditions in the laboratory it is a comparatively easy matter to decide how the work is to be done.   Sometimes extreme measures are to be followed, and under certain circumstances I will not hesitate to use the knife to cut away an adhesion, clip a frænum, or make an incision if the plan adopted requires it.

It is sometimes necessary to go clear away from the denture to build up a depression, and in a late case where there was a large sunken place on the left side of the lower jaw by the bicuspidati, although there were no teeth missing nearer than the second molar, I restored the face to form by connecting plumper and plate with a gold bar, much to the satisfaction of the patient.

The field for the practice of artistic prosthetic dentistry has been a narrow one, confined in its best features to continuous gum work, but it need not be so in the future, for while I admit that there is as yet nothing to equal continuous gum work in appearance, its weight, expense and the difficulties of production bar it from general use. Zylonite, celluloid and pink rubber can be wrought into very presentable dentures, and by much labor I have overcome some of the objections to their use with single teeth. The loosening of single teeth can be prevented by binding the teeth together with platina wire. The labor of modeling the gums in wax, carving them after hardening and the repolishing may be saved by following methods which I will mention.

In order to produce at once a strip of wax shaped like the gums I have carved four moulds in plaster, bordered them with strips of metal and surrounded each mould and metal border with cement— so as to hold them in place (Fig. 15).

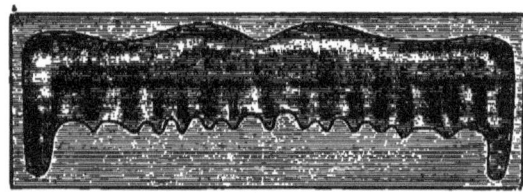

Fig. 15.

In these moulds I press wax which the metal border trims to shape. The elevations, depressions and festoons of the gums are reproduced by the mould so that when the teeth are placed in position and the inequalities of the cast are filled out, the moulded wax may be placed in position by commencing to fit it on the median line and adjusting the parts at the necks of the teeth. If the teeth are unusually large, stretch the wax; if small, crowd it back to fit the spaces. The moulds are finely stippled so that the surface of the plate when finished, does not have little pits in it like those seen, when the stippling is done on the wax model or after the plate is carved.

A method for accurately reproducing the model when carved or moulded has puzzled the dental profession for many years, but now any rubber, celluloid or zylonite plate which has carved and stippled gums, highly finished on all sides, may be placed in a patient's mouth within five minutes after removal from the flask. The work and expense to prepare the models are but trifles, and after the vulcanizing or stamping is done no lathe work is required.

Make all the changes in the impression instead of upon the cast, have it heavily electro-plated with copper or nickel; electro-platers charge me five cents for each copper plate.

If the impression is of beeswax, the electro-plater will prepare it for the bath, if of plaster paris I advise hot waxing, polishing and finally gilding by laying on gold leaf. If you are not accustomed to laying gold leaf, you may have the idea that it is expensive and will require skill to do this part of the work. The expense is nominal, the labor a trifle and the skill ordinary. Forty cents will buy a book of gold which will cover many casts. The only tool necessary is a gilder's tip with which to lift the delicate leaves. If modeling composition is fresh and waxy it will "take" the plumbago like beeswax, but if hard and dry, it also must be gilded.

After the impression has been electro-plated, I fill the shell with plaster and make a die that is better than solid metal for my purpose, because there will be no danger to the plate in removing it after the hardening process. When the wax model is finished ready for investment, place it upon the metallic die and have the carved surfaces heavily electro-plated. Then flask the case in the usual manner, and when the lingual surface of the flask is removed, cut a broad shallow waste gate at the rear only, and electro-plate its entire plaster surface.

When the denture is removed from the flask it will be covered entirely with a thick sheet of copper, and after that is peeled off you will find in their minutest details, reproductions of your cast and model so that if the waste is cut away with a sharp knife, the plate may be placed in the mouth at once.

DISCUSSION.

Dr. Dorrance of Ann Arbor, in opening the discussion said that we have had before us an illustration of the fact that the gentleman who prepared the paper has had an artistic training, and also an illustration of the additional fact, which has been claimed for some years by the profession, that a dentist needs to be an artist, to have his fingers educated to work with brains, and in fact to have several other qualities that are not usually afforded. Dr. Comstock had certainly given the profession some new ideas. He had suggested some simple plans which may be carried out. It was lamentable to contemplate the fact that almost the entire body of the profession at large were ignorant of the subject from a lack of care. He would claim that the dentist, whether he has to practice this branch of the profession or not, should have sufficient knowledge of the subject to intelligently direct those into whose hands he puts his work.

Dr. W. W. Allport of Chicago: These diagrams represented here, only show the necessity of what I have contended for, for years, and that is that men should take up this department of dentistry as an art, as a painter or sculptor takes up his business as an art. Now, we are told that all dentists should learn to make these diagrams and these portraits, and that they should make their artificial substitutes to conform to the proportions, the curves and the different lines that are carried out in the natural face. We are told we ought to do it, and if we do not do it ourselves we should be qualified to direct somebody else to do it. I want to ask each one of the gentlemen here to-night to ask himself this question, "Can I do it, or can I ever learn to do it as an artist?" And we know that there is not one man in twenty that can do it; we know that men who study law, medicine, or theology can never become artists and learn to do what this gentleman has placed before us to-night. Therefore, I say, men should make this department of our practice a specialty, and should follow it; they should have their own offices; they should do their own work in their own way as an artist or painter would do his work.

Dr. L. P. Haskell of Chicago, suggested the feasibility of Dr. Comstock preparing for publication a work embodying in a concise manner his ideas on the subject, so that a copy of it could be placed in the hands of every dentist in America. Some dentists could arrange the teeth satisfactorily as regards the contour of the face and lips, but it was not an easy matter to tell students how to do it. He thought it would be conferring a great favor on the profession if he would proceed to produce such a work.

Dr. Comstock said that with regard to teaching artistic adaptation, he would say that it could be systematized and taught to dental students. He believed that every principle that was applied to art and could be applied to dental practice, had been represented

in some of his articles on the subject.   He had searched to find an
additional principle to be demonstrated.   As far as his knowledge
is concerned, he believes the matter could be so arranged as to be
taught in dental colleges.

The Secretary, in the absence of the essayist, read a paper on

OBTUNDING SENSITIVE DENTINE, AND CONTROLLING PERIDENTAL
INFLAMMATION BY ELECTROLYSIS.

BY D. F. McGRAW, MANKATO, MINN.

With all the wonderful advancement that has been made in the
mechanical department of our profession in the last decade, it
would seem as though an important feature of every-day practice
had been entirely lost sight of, that in our haste to become profi-
cient mechanicians we had entirely forgotten that we were dealing
with human beings, and in the performance of these wonderful
feats of dental skill were causing untold suffering, and doing nothing to alleviate them.

Many different agents have been brought before the profession
whose merits as obtundents of sensitive dentine have been heralded
far and wide, but when placed under the critical test of actual
demonstration have proven failures, except in so far as to draw hard-
earned dollars out of the pockets of the over-zealous members of
the dental profession.

This new system of obtunding dentine, and of controlling peri-
dental inflammation, has this feature in its favor : To begin with, it
is not patented, nor are the drugs and instruments confined to the
control of one house or one combination.   You who are interested
enough to make the necessary outlay can go into the open market
to purchase your outfit and supplies and not feel that you are being
robbed.

The next feature of importance is, that it is absolutely safe, and
no evils can result from its use.

The third is, that it performs all that is claimed for it.

With the discovery of the anæsthetic properties of cocaine, its
virtues were heralded throughout the world ; so great was the
stampede for it that the manufacturers could not begin to supply
the demand.   The consequence was, the price went to a point that
only those in high standing in the profession, from a financial
standpoint, could touch it.   It was shortly discovered, however,
that when it allayed the pain in one sensitive tooth, there were

ninety and nine that failed to respond to its soothing effects, and the profession reluctantly came to the conclusion that they had again been made the dupes of designing manufacturers.

This method that we shall present to you at this meeting, to gain insensibility in teeth, is the following :

To a twelve per cent solution of cocaine add an equal amount of absolute alcohol, making a six per cent solution of cocaine in alcohol.   In connection with this I use the galvanic current, varying the power as the needs of each case may indicate. The method of application is as follows :

First apply the rubber dam; wet a pledget of cotton in the solution, placing it in the cavity of the tooth, pressing the point of the positive pole on to the cotton and the negative pole, with sponge attachment thoroughly wet, to the cheek, turning on the current. Rarely will more than four cells be necessary, if the battery, is in good working order.

An application of three minutes, with an interval of three minutes and then another three-minute application, are sufficient in the majority of cases, although I have to occasionally make the third application, then dry the cavity thoroughly and commence excavating.   My deductions as to the physiological effects are as follows :   The galvanic current acts as a vehicle for conducting the medicinal agents; the cocaine current anæsthetizes the odontoblastic cells and the pulp; the styptic properties of the alcohol acts upon the dentinal fibrils, they being of an albuminous nature, causing contraction and increased density and firmness.

My reasons for drawing these conclusions are these:

I have found that the most sensitive teeth can be obtunded ; that after a certain period of rest sensitiveness returns, but never to that degree that existed before the application of the obtundent. Therefore, I conclude that a change has taken place in the dentinal fibrils, which I maintain is due to the styptic properties of the alcohol, and not to the electrolytic action of the galvanic current. Another reason is, that a tooth in which the pulp is devitalized is a non-conductor of the electric current.   A tooth which had been extracted was subjected to a twelve-cell current of a freshly charged battery and proved an absolute non-conductor.

In the treatment of peri-dental inflammation we have to use a stronger current, for this reason :   It is well known that a strong current will tetanize the vessels, causing a diminished flow of blood

to the parts, thus lessening congestion. The same current, longer
continued, will cause electrolytic decompostion. These are laws of
galvanic electricity that are incontrovertible. The medicinal agents
that I use in all cases of peri-dental inflammation and the blind
abscess are as follows :

A saturated solution of chloride of sodium, seven ounces, tincture of ergot, one ounce. In the chloride of sodium we have one
of the constituents of the blood, where it keeps the fibrine and
albumen in solution. The tissues in an inflamed condition lack
this element, which we supply artificially. In the tincture of ergot
we have a drug that stimulates contraction of the blood vessels,
causing anæmia. Taken together we have here a combination
which decreases the flow of blood, reducing congestion, at the
same time furnishing an element which is lacking and upon the
presence of which normal conditions depend.

The treatment of blind abscess requires stronger battery power,
in order that we may get the full benefit of electrolysis.

Dr. Weeks informs me that he has had remarkable success in
using this method in removing pulps. My experience in this line
has been exceedingly limited, having used it in only two cases.
The first was partially successful and the second was a complete
success. The failure of the first, I attributed to the congested condition of the pulp. I would recommend getting the pulp in a
healthy condition first, as I find that in cases where we have an
inflamed condition, the full anæsthetic effects are not as easily
gained as where the pulp is normal.

In conclusion, I would say, that we have here a compound that
is willing to do our bidding, fulfilling all requirements in the most
satisfactory manner. The satisfaction that our patients will evince will
compensate in more ways than one, for the time spent in thoroughly   ·
investigating it and making ourselves masters of the situation.

You may occasionally find a nervous person who objects to
having a battery used around the mouth for fear of being " shocked,"
but it is easy to calm their fears by an intelligent explanation and
the results that are to crown your efforts by this method of treatment.

The President arose and said: Gentlemen, I thank you for your
full attendance, for your excellent papers and discussions, for your
universal courtesy toward one another while doing so, and for your
generosity and forbearance with your Chairman. (Great applause.)

The Society then adjourned.

CLINICS.

WEDNESDAY MORNING, FEBRUARY 6, 1889.

J. B. VERNON of St. Louis.—A case of permanent bridge-work, extending from the lower first bicuspid to third molar inclusive. This was an unusually favorable case for a typical piece of bridge-work, and it promised to be very useful.

C. THOMAS of Des Moines, Iowa.—Porcelain filling, which was made in the following manner: The cavity, on the labial surface of a superior cuspid, was first prepared with under-cuts, and a thin piece of platinum burnished into it. The platinum formed a matrix, which was then removed and filled with porcelain body and baked. The portion of the filling extending beyond the enamel into the neck was colored to harmonize with the gum. The platinum was ground away on a bevel, so as not to show at the cavity margin, and then it was set with cement.

S. G. PERRY of New York.—A filling of Watts' crystal-gold, using hand mallet and Weber-Perry engine and mallet.

T. E. WEEKS of Minneapolis, Minn.—Original method of investment and soldering.—After assembling the various parts together, ready for soldering, when setting any of the porcelain crowns with a band or ferrule, Dr. Weeks coats the porcelain tooth with oil, and wraps the piece in *moist* asbestos felt foil, leaving exposed only those parts to be soldered. By this means the piece may be immediately soldered, without waiting for the investment to dry; furthermore, the porcelain is better protected from sudden changes in temperature than in any other method of investment, because the asbestos is so excellent a non-conductor. This investment is also applicable in those cases where opal glass or jewelers' white enamel is used in joining Bonwill and other crowns to the bands or collars.

J. W. WICK of St. Louis, Mo. Two gold fillings on mesial surfaces of central incisors, using a hand mallet himself, with a continuous stroke similar to electric mallet.

DR. LOUIS OTTOFY of Chicago.—Implantation.—The patient was twenty-five years of age and of good health. Four years ago the superior left first molar had been extracted, and in the space between the second bicuspid and second molar, there was sufficient vacancy to implant a bicuspid. A flap of the gum was made by cutting this tissue in a semi-circle from the second bicuspid to

the second molar, and being raised from the bone it was held in
that position while the socket was prepared. This was made with
the Younger, Walker and Ottofy trephines, socket-knives, and crib-
knives. The tooth, which during the operation was kept in a solution of bichloride of mercury, one part to one thousand of water,
was frequently inserted and the socket made as near as possible to
fit the root of the tooth. Some difficulty was experienced by cutting down the septa of bone, which at one time separated the roots
of the molar (previously occupying this space) from each other.
The tooth once in place, and properly articulated, after perfect
sterilization of the tooth and of the cell prepared for its reception,
was held *in situ* by a cap of gold and platinum plate about thirty-
three standard guage. The retention cap covered the implanted
tooth, and each of its neighbors; it was cemented in place with
oxyphosphate cement.

THURSDAY MORNING, FEBRUARY 7.

DR. C. N. JOHNSON of Chicago.—Gold filling.—A superior right
first bicuspid, having a distal cavity extending into the fissure of
the crown. The filling was introduced with the usual pluggers,
and the aid of the hand mallet. The Brophy matrix and the Ivory
clamps were adjuncts during the operation. The cervical border
was protected with Pack's semi-cohesive gold rolls. In the remain-
der of the cavity the gold foil used was previously annealed.

DR. E. H. ALLEN of Freeport, Ill.—Gold filling, using electric
mallet.—Two cavities were filled with No. 4 cohesive foil, folded
until it would have the thickness of No. 64. The cavities were situated on the distal surface of the superior left cuspid, and the mesial surface of the superior left first bicuspid. The operator annealed all the gold used in these cavities, and hence the margins
of the cavity, as well as the central portions, were filled with cohesive
gold.

DR. C. W. LEWIS of Chicago.—Gold filling, Herbst method.—A
large cavity in the inferior left second molar was filled with Pack's
crown pellets. They are used soft for the commencement of the operation, the soft pellets having been placed into the cavity and covered with a pellet of cotton, the mass of gold is burnished into all of
the inequalities of the cavity and especially to its margins. In this
way a perfect adaptation of the gold to the margin is obtained. The
central portion of the cavity, being largely exposed to mastication,

was filled with the same gold, but in a semi-cohesive condition, and the surface was also finished with the same gold, cohesive, and by the aid of the mallet. All of the burnishers are of steel and are used with the engine and by hand, while the instruments used for filling the central and exposed portions of the cavity are those of the usual make and patterns.

DR. MARVIN E. SMITH of Chicago.—Gold filling, using Snow and Lewis plugger.—This operator filled a compound cavity, extending over the crown and distal surface of a superior right first molar. No. 4 gold foil was used in a soft condition while in proximity to the margins of the cavity, and annealed when in the central and exposed portions. The condensation of the gold throughout was made with the Snow and Lewis plugger.

DR. E. M. S. FERNANDEZ of Chicago.—Oxyphosphate cement filling.—After the cavity has been prepared in the usual manner for the reception of a plastic filling, the tooth and cavity being perfectly dry, the assistant mixes the cement, at first quite thin; this is then pressed into the cavity with ivory or wooden instruments. Thicker mixtures of the mass are then introduced and with it the thinner portions displaced and pressed out of the cavity. Continue in this mannner until finally the filling is finished with very thickly mixed cement. The surface of the filling is then dried with steel instruments and the powder of the cement. In a few minutes the powder from the surface of the filling should be brushed away with a camel's hair brush, to be followed by thoroughly rubbing it with cotton dipped in sandarac varnish. As soon as the varnish is dry, the rubber-dam can be removed. All of the instruments used should be scrupulously clean, and the filling should be finished in such a way that there is no cutting away or polishing of the surface of the filling, the latter should be polished and made perfectly smooth by the pressure of the instruments used.

DR. E. A. ROYCE of Chicago, inserted a gold filling in the inferior right first molar, mesial surface, using Abbey's non-cohesive gold in cylinders prepared by himself. The cylinders contain one-third to one-half sheet of gold rolled very tight, and are used principally in starting and filling the body of the cavity. Gold in tape form or loose pellets for the upper and masticating surface. Rapidity and ease of insertion, together with perfect adaptation, is claimed for this method, which the operator well demonstrated.

DR. C. THOMAS of Des Moines, Iowa, finished the porcelain

inlay inserted at the previous clinic. The shade of color might have been a trifle closer, but the operation, taken altogether, was the best of its kind yet seen by the reporter.

DR. J. B. VERNON of St. Louis, Mo., completed the bridge piece begun on Wednesday for Dr. Cormany. It proved a perfect piece of workmanship, light and cleanly. Dr. Vernon also exhibited a set of instruments for driving on bands, crowns, etc. These instruments consist of steel handles, bent at different angles, with socket at the tip for holding a boxwood plug. A device for holding and sifting plaster was also shown by the same person, and it has the appearance of being a very useful adjunct to the laboratory. The dies for the hollow gold crowns which composed the bridge piece were also made after a peculiar design of his own.

The removable bridge, specimens shown by DR. T. S. WATERS of Baltimore, Md., are held in position by means of springs, and offers advantages that will amply repay investigation. In one case, the use of split posts in the roots of several teeth, as a retaining force exhibited one method of attachment. Other cases, where live teeth were present, a gold cap with a half round groove at the side, in which fitted springs made from half round gold wire, showed another method.

J. W. WASSALL.—Canal-filling.—The canals of two lower molars were filled with gutta-percha in the usual manner, except that in the canals of the anterior root, being smaller in calibre, the chloro-percha solution was followed by a tapered gold wire filling instead of gutta-percha cones. There is no advantage claimed for the gold wire other than that it can be more certainly pushed to the extremity of the canal carrying with it the liquid gutta-percha. By this method the necessity for enlarging canals with drills is avoided. The broaches used in this clinic were filed out of platinum gold wire (standard gauge No. 24), a suggestion of Dr. H. J. McKellops.

The operation of DR. WICK of St. Louis, the restoration of contour in the two superior central incisors, was open to inspection, and well bore the closest scrutiny.

J. G. REID of Chicago.—Demonstrated the use of copper amalgam in filling two cavities; one situated on the mesial surface of an upper right first molar, and the second cavity on the distal surface of adjoining bicusped. Immediate separation of the teeth was accomplished by the use of Dr. R. B. Winder's separator. The ease with which this appliance can be adjusted, the rapidity with which it does the work at a minimum expense of pain, seems to recommend it at once as being an instrument of general utility.

(See cut and description under the head of "New Appliances.")

A. H. THOMPSON of Topeka, Kas.—Gum colored porcelain, inlay filling.—Cavity on labial surface of neck and root of upper pulpless cuspid. Two pieces of porcelain gum from block teeth were fitted in cavity, the outer edges beveled to fit underneath. The pieces were fitted together in the median line to form the proper contour. The inlays were then colored to correspond with gum and tooth and set according to the method described in his paper.

DR. T. L. GILMER of Quincy, Illinois, exhibited gold crowns, made by himself, which are telescoped over platinum bands, made to fit the root exactly. Also a combination crown of platinum and Weston's metal; and of gold, porcelain and Weston's metal.

The attention of the reporters of THE DENTAL REVIEW was called to the mal-position of the various operators, while at the chair. At clinics, the operators may be partially excused, because of unfamiliarity with the chair and the necessarily altered condition of the surroundings. If more attention were given to this subject by the operator in his own office, possibly the average life of the dentist, now about 40 years, might be considerably increased. Defective optics, round shoulders and pulmonary diseases may become less frequently the ailments of the dentist. One operator was in a position, wherein it was out of the question for him to allow a free passage of the respired air, into and out of one of the lungs, while the muscles of the other, were in a continued state of tension, thus preventing the interchange of the gases in the remote parts of the lung tissue, because the free mobility of the lung had been interfered with. Another was observed to throw his entire weight on one foot, causing the muscles of one leg to support and balance the body, when a slight elevation of the chair would have prevented the unnecessary exertion. However, he soon obviated the necessity of using the other leg, by leaning with his elbow on the patient's stomach. One operator, standing at the side, a little to the front of the chair, had much difficulty in securing proper access to manipulate in the cavity of a lower tooth. It necessitated the extension of the arm, into a position consiting of angles at the shoulder, elbow, wrist and finger joints ; the operator's appearance was painful to the observer and there must have been unusual fatigue to the operator—lowering the chair and standing behind and a little to the left of the head-rest would have been a pleasant position to enable the operator to work with ease. We merely call the attention of dentists to this subject for the purpose of having them give some thought to it, and by a slight consideration of it, to remedy any errors of this kind, of which they may be conscious.

The practical bridge-piece inserted by DR. PARR of New York City, although the principle is good, did not do the operator justice. The case was a bad one, and a faulty articulation made matters a little worse. We hope to see DR. PARR under more favorable circumstances.

DR. HARLAN removed serumal deposit from several inferior incisors and DR. BLACK wired the same loosened teeth, using gold wire and figure of 8 suture.

NEW APPLIANCES.

Dr. E. M. S. FERNANDEZ of Chicago.—Improvement on the Suspension Dental Engine.—This improvement consists of separating the hand-piece from the speed-knob and inserting between them S. S. White's duplex spring connector, a tubular arm through which a shaft is journaled, one end bearing on each extremity. If a section was made it would show internally, S. S. White's hand-piece, connected with duplex spring and shaft. The latter has one bearing at each end and connects with the speed-knob. *Externally* is the hand-piece connecting with the duplex spring cover, the tubular arm and the speed-knob. The top pulley (for the purpose of suspension) is suspended by a cord run through a pulley attached to the ceiling, another pulley is attached to the corner of the window frame, the cord passing over this, down to the spring or weight on the window sill. When the engine is not in use the arm is hung on a hook on the wall or window sash.

DR. GEO. W. WHITEFIELD of Evanston, Illinois.—Instantaneous break, on dental engine.—The engine exhibited has a great range of motion, can be moved out of the way readily, and by the sudden break of the revolutions of the instrument, can be stopped almost instantaneously, enabling the operator to make a few revolutions only, at a time, if so desired. The break is set by the foot of the operator. The speed is all the way from 600 to 7,000 per minute. The great range of the arm, makes it possible to extend the hand-piece to two, or even three chairs, by swinging the arm. In dental colleges, this feature of the apparatus may be of considerable value.

The burs are cut in a way which prevents any but the cutting edge to touch those portions of the tooth which are being cut, hence friction is obviated and heating of the tooth, even when the instrument is revolving rapidly, partially or wholly obviated.

The Hahn Duplex dental engine and pneumatic mallet, combining mallet and engine in one, was also on exhibition. The engine arm is readily disconnected and when this is done the engine operates only the mallet, by keeping in motion an air-pump, the air being transmitted through a rubber tube to the hand-piece. The action of the mallet is similar to the action of pneumatic mallets. When the engine arm is connected and the mallet arm disconnected, the apparatus is then simply a dental engine.

The root-dryer of Dr. J. H. Wooley of Chicago, was also on exhibition and its practicability fully demonstrated.

An apparatus for disinfecting instruments was exhibited by Dr. C. J. Peterson of Dubuque, Iowa. It comprised a small copper tank for heating water to which a disinfectant had been added, and a wire gauze tray with handle, with which to submerge the instruments. The inventor claimed many advantages for the apparatus, viz.: Absolute cleanliness and thorough disinfection; hot water always ready at a minute's notice, in softening gutta-percha easily without fear of over heating, and finally the influence on the patient who sees all the instruments submitted to a bath before using upon another person.

A beautiful specimen of porcelain inlay, set in gold, was exhibited as the work of Dr. A. W. Hoyt of Chicago.

Dr. Call of Peoria presented a seamless platinum tube for use in Dunn's Medicinal syringe.

A shield of metal about two inches in diameter, on which a piece of emery cloth or paper is laid, the two being placed on a mandril and used with the dental engine, was exhibited by Dr. ———— ———— The device used for sharpening tools, is simple and convenient. Similar shields have been used for years with the dental engine for the purpose of supporting sand-paper and emery-paper discs when used in the mouth. The paper thus supported by the shield answers the purposes of an emery wheel, it is, however, thin and flexible.

DR. J. J. R. PATRICK of Belleville, Ill., exhibited a combination tool for preparing gold screw plugs and posts, and the making of gold broaches, which he cannot get on the market any too soon for those dentists who practice gold crown work, or, in fact, any operation requiring screw posts. The instrument is shaped like an ordinary pair of pliers, but upon its upper surface is inserted a hardened steel knife-edge tapering groove, by which the gold wire may be shaved down to a fine tapering point ; between the jaws, on either side, are two screw plates, in which is laid the wire, already trimmed in the shaper, when with a reverse motion and gentle pressure on the handles, the wire is withdrawn and shows a fine screw thread cut on its surface. A cutting jaw a little behind the flat portion of the pliers enables one to cut the post to the required length. In the tip of the jaw is a set screw, and at the side of set screw is a small chisel blade standing at an angle to the under surface, and a small opening in this under surface gives an opportunity for passing in a fine gold wire which may be barbed with the chisel above. We are really at a loss to know if the above description fully enumerates all the points of this wonderful tool. It must be seen to be appreciated.

DR. R. B. WINDER'S SEPARATOR AND RUBBER-DAM CLAMP.

The above cut represents a new appliance designed to be used either as a separator or a rubber-dam clamp. Its chief advantages are self-adjusting, easily and quickly applied, and when in position is not in the way of the operator.

The jaws of the clamp and also the wedges for separating are interchangeable, so that the operator can select such sizes as are suitable for the case in hand.

DR. C. F. HARTT of Chicago, gives a rubber handle to pluggers and excavators by coating the steel with rubber and then vulcanizing.

DR. E. A. ROYCE of Chicago, showed a new plugger point which terminates in a serrated ball as per cut, instrument made by S. S. White.

DR. DUNN has greatly increased the efficacy of his medicinal syringe by means of a spring guage attachment, by which the rubber bulb can be compressed and drops measured, which also prevents the liquid from being drawn back into the syringe.

BYRNES' ENGINE PLUGGER.—The instrument has a set-nut for giving a light or heavy blow. Instantaneous increase of the blow is had by pressing the point of the instrument on the filling. To stop the blow altogether push the latch-pin in, at the same time press upon the point of the instrument. While the instrument is pressed back release the latch-pin and it is locked out of gear. Pressure upon the latch-pin will immediately throw it back into gear. In operating the instrument, leave the latch-pin perfectly free to obtain the best results.

Should the engine run backwards it will run the top nut off; to catch it up again it will be necessary to throw the instrument out of gear, and run the engine forward.

By allowing the end of mandril to come out as far as extreme end of clasp there is no trouble in getting hand-piece to grasp the mandril. Snow and Lewis points fit the plugger.

DR. W. H. TAGGART of Freeport, Ill., exhibited a new arrangement of the suspension engine and a device for shaping the ends of roots for crown-bands. The engine is suspended from the ceiling in such a way as to avoid the use of a fusee to raise and lower it to bring it within the proper range for the operator, as the hand piece has a range of four feet in every direction before there is any necessity for a change in the height of pulley-head. This is accomplished by having the pulley-head, which is attached to a Shaw arm, or Hood & Reynolds arm, or S. S. W. cable, balanced in such a way as to cause the belt to always come on the pulley at such an angle as to do away almost entirely with guides so that the only revolving part of the engine is the pulley and cable. No noise from the rattling of guides. In balancing it in this way there is no drag to the hand piece and absolutely no weight except that of the hand-piece.

The engine is intended to run by an electric or other motor, placed in an adjoining room. Dr. Taggart has his run by 60 feet of belt. The longer the belt the smoother it runs. In this way all the noise can be confined to an adjoining room, and as the engine itself runs absolutely noiseless we have the perfection of a power engine in the operating room. This can also be run by a foot treadle the same as any other suspension engine.

The root-trimmer consists of a pin cemented into the root which acts as a bearing on which the trimmer proper revolves and also give the direction in which the shoulder is to be trimmed.

The trimmer consists of a hollow flexible drill made by having a series of special shaped steel or other spring-lips set in a circle the only object of these lips is to hold the abrasive powder, which does the cutting, in contact with the outside of the root. The flexible springs are intended to follow the general outline of the root and to take off just enough of the root to make the sides parallel and not to cut a decided shoulder.

The general outline of the root is preserved and the same instrument will parallel the sides of a round, oval or pear shaped root without taking off any more material than enough to get the root properly shaped.

Another advantage is this — as the root is trimmed entirely in the direction in which the pin is set, in bridge work it is only necessary to set the two or more pins in the different roots parallel with each other, and the roots will be the same when trimmed, thus overcoming any difficulty in having the bridge go to place.

THE BANQUET.

The banquet was the crowning feature. It was well attended. After all the members and invited guests had filed into the large dining-room, and taken their seats, Dr. Noyes invoked divine blessing, following which came the feast. The next thing in order was the ventilation of the post-prandial eloquence that had accumulated in each bosom, and the President arose and spoke as follows:

Invited Guests of the Chicago Dental Society: We bid you a cordial welcome to this our banquet board, that we may for a few hours more enjoy your society, and give us an opportunity to express our heartfelt thanks to you for your many generous efforts toward making our twenty-fifth anniversary meeting a success. The presents that you have brought to this, our silver wedding, are priceless, and will be treasured by each member. In your wanderings around our city you have doubtless seen many things of interest of which we are justly proud. It is not my purpose to boast to you of our tall buildings, our street railways, our tunnels and bridges, our beautiful parks and boulevards, and our Mayor (Applause), but there is one thing of which I will boast—that is the great love the Chicago dentist has in his heart towards every progressive dentist throughout the land. (Applause.) If "brevity is the soul of wit," I think I have considerable wit. (Great laughter.)

The President: The first toast of the evening reads like this: 'Hereto we have invited many a guest such as we love." I will call upon Dr. T. E. Weeks, of Minneapolis, Minn., to respond to this toast.

Dr. Weeks said : *Mr. President and Brethren of the Dental Profession*—I have not language to express the feelings that possess me at this time in being honored with an invitation to respond to that toast. Chicago is a great city. This is a great meeting; it is a great attendance; it has a great President. (Laughter and applause.) I think I voice the sentiments of every visiting dentist when I speak of the reciprocal feeling, of the pleasure that your President, Dr. Swasey, took of notifying us to hear him. I do not think the love of the Chicago dentists is any bigger than that the visiting members have for the Chicago Dental Society. I know a few of us from the State of Minnesota have a warm feeling for Chicago. We are attracted here very often by numerous good things that your President spoke of. I suppose he enumerated all the attractions. (Laughter.) Minnesota is a great State in a good many ways, and it has good dentists, and they are pretty good fellows, and they would like to have the opportunity to entertain as they are being entertained now. There are a good many attractions aside from dentists. I call to mind that at our table the conversation turned on shooting and hunting. Dentists, as a rule, are fond of that kind of sport. I have the best authority for the story I am about to relate in regard to the kind of shooting we have in Minnesota. We have a peculiar breed of ducks up there. The story, as related to me, was as follows:

The speaker said he was out south of the city one afternoon strolling along to see if he couldn't shoot a duck or two. There were some black heads flying over him and he was fortunate enough to wound one. You all know that when the sun is in the right direction you see all that is beneath the water on a little elevation, but the wounded duck fell into the water, and it was that particular brand of ducks which dive. He said he kept watching the place where the duck went down, and he suddenly discovered the duck swimming toward him, and in the direction where there were two points of comparatively solid earth that approached each other within about two feet. He watched the duck swimming towards these two points of land. He got there before the duck did and threw himself prostrate on the ground, put his hand into the water, the duck swam into his hands, and he put it in his bag. With that kind of accommodating game to offer you as an inducement, in addition to the hearty good fellowship that we may extend to you, we hope that each and every man will honor Minnesota with a visit. I do not think you had all better come at once, there may not be ducks enough to go around. (Laughter.) But seriously, gentlemen, while on this phase of the subject, we do expect to have a meeting of the Minnesota State Dental Society next summer, and in behalf of the dentists of our State I extend a cordial and personal invitation to you all to come and meet with us. The meeting will be held in Duluth, and I assure you that everything will be done to entertain you that the poor people of Minnesota can do. I think you would have a good time, as we predict a good meeting.

The occasion here has been one of the most enjoyable to me I have ever attended. It has been my good fortune to attend a number of dental meetings in the last few years; but there are some features of this meeting that have struck me forcibly and impressively, and I wish to speak of them. It has been a meeting for business. There has been no opportunity for politics or wrangling, of any kind, and we have got all the good out of the meeting that we could get. (Applause.) I certainly think the class of papers that are introduced in dental meetings now are by all odds an improvement on those of a few years back. As far as good fellowship of the meetings is concerned, that certainly is not growing less. I, for one, am proud to say that the best friends I have in the world are dentists. (Applause.) I would not have it otherwise. I feel it is an honor to be able to say that. It is an honor for any one to say that the dearest friends he has in the world are his confreres throughout the country, who are engaged in the same line of work that he is. I think we are growing closer and closer together as we go on. I believe we are doing a good work, and the profession as a profession is rapidly improving. While I do not think I could talk connectedly all night, yet I am "full" enough to do so. (Great laughter.) I will not occupy any more of your time as I know the committee must have other good things to offer. I thank you for all the courtesies I have had, and especially this last and greatest of all. (Applause.)

To the toast, "The Pioneers of the Profession," Dr. W. W. Allport of Chicago, made the following response: *Mr. President and Gentlemen:* I am very glad to be called upon as a young man to respond to this toast, as had I been addressed by the Chair as an old man I would not have been proud. To speak of the pioneers in the dental profession, it can hardly be that you mean *me*, Mr. President; I am not even one of them. The pioneers are nearly all dead. If my memory refers back to the time I first practiced, I think of those old pioneers who commenced when we had little literature; there are but few, especially such men as Harris, Townsend, Gunning, Harwood, Keep and others, who had given us the commencement or foundation upon which we have established our literature and practice, and I was then a young man. I remember attending one of the largest meetings ever known in the world amongst dentists a few years after I had entered practice. It was held in a little hall in New York city. There were a little less than 200 members present, and these men were gathered from all over this broad land from one part to the other. They comprised the best men of the profession at that time, and perhaps the best men in the world. Now, here to-night I see before me men fully as able as those we had at that time, and nearly all gathered from a small section of country. Whilst these gentlemen laid the foundation for our practice and literature, the men here this evening have come along one after another working in the interests of the profession; and while I know I look old, I can hardly say I feel old. I am as young in feeling as any other member. (Applause.) That is, I feel just as anxious and enthusiastic in regard to the future of dentistry now, and more so than I did at that time. At that time we had but one dental college in the whole land, and we kept growing and growing, but during all this time we, the older practitioners, whilst growing old and gray, I believe, without exception, were just as young and enthusiastic for the future of our profession, and looked forward with great pride for its future advancement; because we knew more what we ought to be and what intelligent people expect of us by and by. We feel the enthusiasm; we know the American spirit of what we ought to be will be, and are going to be sometime. With the number of colleges we have, with all the dental literature at our disposal, the object of every man in practice should be never to grow old, but always feel young, and be a pioneer in the true sense of keeping abreast of all that is going on, gathering the best thoughts pertaining to his profession from all sources, and if we keep young and steady, keep looking out for the grand future that awaits us, there is no reason why we should grow old in spirit. I have said enough. I thank you Mr. President. (Applause).

To the toast, "The Dental Press," Dr. W. X. Sudduth of Philadelphia, arose and spoke as follows :

Mr. President and Gentlemen : A serious subject. This is a subject that can not be discussed in a way that would be a fitting accompaniment to an after dinner speech. I cannot take up the subject without feeling impressed with its seriousness—without feeling impressed as I look over the faces of those before me, and feeling that we are building monuments; that we, here assembled, are the men who are to make the dental press what it will be in the future, not those who stand at the helm, but those who fill its columns. Our dental journals can not be, or never will rise, higher than the source from which they receive their supply. I have been most highly entertained at this meeting; the scientific character of the papers presented have filled me with pleasure from the first to the last. As mentioned by Dr. Weeks, there has been such a marked advancement in the character of our papers and dental literature that no one can look over and note the advancement that has been made in our journals without feeling that there is a grand stride being made in this direction. As I look into your faces and see the expression of enthusiasm that has attended this entire meeting, I feel highly encouraged to pick up and go on with this good work, and I know my confrères of the press, several of whom are present with us here this evening, have received a stimulus from this meeting as well as every meeting that has taken place in the last few years. We look to you, gentlemen, for support in the building up of our journals; without that support we can not do ourselves justice, or do justice to you. We look to you for the material which goes into the monuments we are building, and the character of our journals will be exactly as you give us the material. (Applause.)

In response to the toast, "A Quarter Century of the Chicago Dental Society." Dr. Geo. H. Cushing of said Chicago, said :

Mr. President : It is perhaps one of the penalties of advancing years that I have been selected to respond to this toast. I will only refer to some of the phases of this society's existence since twenty-five years ago. Dr. Allport, and every other gentlemen like himself, were impressed with the importance of organizing a society in this city, and we gathered together and succeeded in getting enough to form the nucleus of the society you see to-day. The younger men of the profession have no conception of the difficulties under which we labored. As I look back upon the obstructions that were placed in our way, and then look upon the society that we see before us to-day, it is surprising that we succeeded as we did under so many trials and tribulations. We have now reached a high standing, and, as my friend Dr. Allport has said, while we may look old and gray, we do not feel old, and are not old, professionally. We are looking with hope upon the younger and rising members of the profession who are gathered here. After taking a retrospective view of these many years, as some of us can, we can not but predict a future full of promise. (Applause.)

To the toast, "The City of Chicago, the Professional Center of the West," the Hon. John A. Roche, Mayor, arose amid much applause and spoke as follows :

Mr. President and Gentlemen : I am very glad to be with you, although I must confess that I was not prepared to keep my appointment to-night much better than when I make an appointment with Dr. Brophy. I felt inclined to be here, but, as usual, I was busy and had forgotten I had an engagement. It is very convenient for me to forget when I have an engagement with my friend on the right (meaning Dr. Brophy) ; I suppose that is the trouble with a good many of those who go to a dentist's office.

Your President says that you love each other. Well, it is well that you do love each other. (Laughter.) I do not want to say anything in the presence of the doctor.

Our friend (meaning Dr. Weeks) from Minnesota extended a kind invitation to you to visit the Northwest. I would be glad to go with you ; I am fond of fishing and hunting, and all of the pleasures we may find in Minnesota ; but the kind of ducks that the dentists have in Chicago are lame ducks. (Laughter.) We

can not say much about game just now; we find it very difficult to
have a very large game.

The gentleman who spoke of the pioneers reminded me of
twenty-five years ago when a boy in Massachusetts. A dentist
informed me, or rather said to a lady friend when I was present,
"Here is a boy, who, when he is twenty years of age won't have any
teeth." How is it, doctor? (referring to Dr. Brophy.) I am not
very old, but I am more than twenty, and I believe I have pretty
nearly all of my teeth at the present time, but I changed dentists.
(Laughter.) Should I criticise him? I think not. Remember
that was only twenty-five years ago. It was in a little town. He
did the best he could with the information he had. He didn't use
a ladle and pour it in; he did everlastingly hurt when he was ham-
mering it in. It was not the expensive stuff we have to pay for now.
(Roars of laughter.) But is it expensive? When you want a good
thing you must pay for it. If you would have a good painting you
must purchase it from a good artist. If you would have any first-
class work done it must be done by one who is skilled in the profession. The use of the hand, the eye, and the close attention that
the dentist must necessarily pay to his business is something that
we who do not practice can not help noticing. He fabricates something that we can use; and to the gentlemen of this profession I
must say that I am surprised at the advancement that has been
made in dentistry. (Applause.) With electricity going up into our
eight and ten-story buildings, 175 feet above the sidewalk, with the
electric engine and all the new apparatus that you now have, we in
Chicago may well look forward to being a great center. While in
company with a gentleman to-day we talked about the time
when we would have a population of two million and a half—
there are no St. Louis people here, I suppose. (Loud and prolonged laughter.) Now, if we have these two million and a half
of people, and they continue to eat food without any special regard
for their teeth, how many teeth would there be to take care of in
the city of Chicago? That is a mathematical problem that I would not
be able to figure out. But there will be more teeth to be filled if the
members of this profession continue to diligently pursue their work,
and to do it in such a way as to benefit humanity. I hope that when
our city arrives at that point when we will have such a large number of people that we will also have good dental colleges, as well
as educated, honest, earnest, reliable men, and that the people who

visit the gentlemen engaged in this profession will have more regard for their promises and try to keep their engagements better than myself. (Applause.)

Gentlemen, I am glad to welcome you to our city. I am glad to say to you that we feel proud not only of Chicago, but of the Northwest. We feel proud of the dental societies we have here ; we hope they will increase in number, and it will give me great pleasure at any time to attend your dinners, and I will try to come early. (Applause).

Dr. Hanks of Dubuque, Iowa, on rising to leave the banquet-hall to catch a train, said in a few well-chosen words, he had listened with marked attention to the highly interesting papers and discussions at the different sessions of the Society, and desired to express his thanks for being so cordially and royally entertained.

In response to the toast, "The Illinois State Dental Society, most of whose Members have Graced this Occasion by their Presence," Dr. C. B. Rohland of Alton, its former President, spoke as follows:

Mr. President and Gentlemen:—It is said that "Out of the fulness of the heart the mouth speaketh." The Illinois State Dental Society I will not attempt to eulogize. She has done good work. She points with pride to her past. The occasion which we have been celebrating together here is a great success. The Chicago Dental Society has reason to be proud of it, but the Illinois State Dental Society is still prouder, and why ? Because it feels that the energy and labor that have brought success here is largely due to the inspiration received from her. She is proud of it because she finds that the bone and sinew of the Chicago Dental Society, which has produced this grand success is largely the bone of her bone and flesh of her flesh. We feel that the success here only points to the anniversary which we hope to celebrate in May, and at which meeting we hope to see everyone who is now here present. We can not help but frankly acknowledge the aid we have received from our neighbors. I see before me the faces of several (out-of-town) members of our State Society, and when our annual meeting comes around, we look forward to their attendance with pleasurable expectation, and I am glad to have this opportunity to express this obligation.

Dr. L. C. Ingersoll of Keokuk, Iowa, in responding to the toast, "Brotherly Love, the Foundation of Ethics," spoke substantially as follows:

Mr. President and Gentlemen: I thank you for this grand demonstration. Dentists of the West, of the North, and of the South, around the banquet table, we owe our thanks to the Chicago Dental Society for inaugurating the occasion for this magnificent demonstration. One of the greatest teachers the world has ever known has said, " Love is the fulfilling of the law, the law of human relation, the relation of man to man, and the relation of man to his God." No man has any right to offer his professional services to his fellow-man unless he has, deep down in his heart of hearts, brotherly love, good-will toward his fellows. Codes of ethics exist in the very nature of man. It is a human relation. I am bound to brotherly love, not by the code of the Illinois State Dental Society or any other society in the world, but because I am a man among men, and for no other reason. I am bound to love it, bound to regard its necessities as equivalent to my own. (Applause.)

Owing to the low tone of voice in which Dr. Ingersoll made his remarks, it was impossible for the stenographer to make a verbatim report of what he said.

To the toast, " Our Benefactors, the Ladies, God Bless Them," Dr. C. C. Chittenden of Madison, Wis., made the following response : I am satisfied that Dr. Swasey selected me to respond to this toast on account of my great similarity to himself, both mentally and physically. (Laughter.) It is a subject which I am utterly incompetent to deal with. If there were ladies here, I might, perhaps, be moved to speak more eloquently than I can possibly do under the circumstances.

Dr. Ingersoll has just spoken of brotherly love, which should actuate us in our actions toward one another; we must do them some good. Brotherly love is instilled into us from childhood by our mothers and those of the other sex with whom we are often thrown in contact. A dentist who does not possess this love can not do the best, the kindest and the most useful thing in ministering to his suffering patient. That, I think, we have all seen in our experience. We are sometimes brought in contact with patients of antagonistic temperament, where it is impossible fo do them good; unless we approach them with a womanly feeling, which all dentists should possess in order to gain the confidence of their patients, we can not help them. We owe a great deal to woman. I believe it was Martin Luther who said, " *Wer nicht liebt Wein, Weib und Gesang, Bleibt ein Narr sein Leben lang,*" which, being liberally interpreted by a German friend of mine, means that "A man that don't love his wife, wine and good singing is a d—d fool as long as he lives." (Roars of laughter, followed by loud and prolonged applause.)

The toast, "Our Profession," was responded to by Dr. J. N. Crouse, who spoke at great length in a humorous way.

The President: We will vary the programme slightly and will now listen to "Poets and Poetry," by Dr. H. J. McKellops of St. Louis. The first poem was entitled "The Ivy and the Oak," which was recited with pleasing effect. The second was entitled, "Beautiful Waters." At the close of the recitations Dr. McKellops was warmly applauded.

To the toast, "Our Friends in the South," Dr. H. W. MORGAN of Nashville, Tennessee, said: *Mr. President and Gentlemen:* In response to this toast I am somewhat at a loss how to express myself. There are but a few men from the South here, many of them are detained on account of various circumstances, some by infirmity, others have heard of your cold winters; but when they read the proceedings of this meeting they will regret very much their absence.

I was much impressed with the words of the gentleman who responded to the toast, "The Pioneers of Dentistry," and in this connection I may point to the history of dentistry in the South. The South gave the profession the first dental college, the first dental journal, and the first dental law. (Applause). While we may not be as active in introducing new inventions, new methods or new investigations, I think I may say that our Southern friends are not behind in making use of them. It is with pride that I assure you that our associations are endeavoring to do as earnest work as you are, and while the late President of the Illinois State Dental Society made the remark that the members of this society had a kind feeling toward the societies of adjoining States, you will pardon me, Mr. President, when I say, we have not had the pleasure of seeing your faces with us. The doors of the South are open to you. No ice locks her bounds. You are cordially invited, one and all. Our hospitality and courtesy are only limited to our opportunities to extend them. The next meeting of the Tennessee State Dental Association will be held at Jackson on the Illinois Central Railway, and we trust that not a few who are here to-night may be present on that occasion. I thank you, gentlemen, for this courteous recognition of the men of the South. (Applause.)

The President called upon Hon. C. K. OFFIELD to respond to the toast: "The Legal Aspects of our Profession."

He said if he read history correctly in his earlier days, there were three learned professions—namely, theology, medicine and law, but within the last quarter of a century there had been a ramification of the profession of medicine, and that is the profession of dentistry, closely allied to·it, and which in his opinion was one of the component parts which goes to make a complete unit in that profession. And then, too, during the last fifty years medicine has been divided into other component parts. There are now specialists on the eye and ear, the nose and throat, etc., etc.

In referring to the Dental Protective Association, and its relations to the Tooth Crown Company, Attorney OFFIELD said : "Of the professions I know of, the dental profession is the only one that takes out a patent. I know of no member of the theological profession that takes out a patent for the best means of saving the souls of sinners or the evangelization of the earth. I know of no member of the legal profession who takes out a patent for the practice of law, and I think I am safe in stating that no member of the medical profession takes out a patent on any process or discovery he may make."

Dr. A. H. THOMPSON of Topeka, Kansas, responded to the toast, "Dental Literature." During the course of his remarks he said there were two important divisions : (1) Text-books, which classified the knowledge for dental colleges, and (2) the periodical publications which promulgated new discoveries and the current thought of the profession.

Dr. T. W. BROPHY of Chicago, in responding to the toast "The Young Men of the Profession," said : *Mr. President, and Gentlemen:* I am glad the toast has been so announced, because I am one of those who believe that we are a profession. We are not only a profession, but we draw from each of the collateral sciences ; and not only from these sciences, but the arts as well. I have quite an acquaintance with the younger men of the profession, and I sometimes wonder whether those who have recently commenced practice become discouraged at failures they have made, and whether they wonder how it is that their fellow practitioners of the same age seem to avoid certain blunders—how they seem to be

more prosperous in their profession. If they do they should con-
sole themselves with the fact that men engaged in all the voca-
tions of life have failures. Failure is not confined to the profession
of dentistry alone. The young men of our profession have very
much to be thankful for. They have the advantage of youth, of
strength; they have the advantage of the failures and successes
that have been made by their predecessors; they have the advantage of better facilities for acquiring a knowledge of their profession
than those who preceded them.

We have listened to remarks here this evening by those who
have spoken of the history and advancement that has been made
in dental literature, journalism, and by the pioneers of the profession. For all the privileges we enjoy we are indebted to the
pioneers in our profession; the men who have labored and deprived
themselves of many things for the sake of advancing the standard of
the profession, and as we have plucked the fruit of their planting, we
should all in thankfulness plant for others yet to be. (Great applause.)

To the toast, "Our Absent Friends, that keep the word of
Promise to our Ear, and Break it to our Hope," Dr. A. W. HARLAN
of Chicago, said: *Mr. President and Gentlemen:* I think that we
all feel sure that even though some of our friends may be absent,
yet they are all with us in spirit, and I call upon one and all of you
to drink with me to our absent friends. (Applause.)

Here every member and guest arose and drank to the health of
those that were absent.

Dr. McKELLOPS arose and proposed that every one drink to the
success of the Chicago Dental Society, which was done.

The President, after thanking the gentlemen for the close and
marked attention with which they had listened to the post-prandial
speeches, called upon the orchestra to render "Home, Sweet Home,"
during which every one arose and participated.

The anniversary meeting, host and guests, then quietly dispersed.

ERRATA.

Dr. Martindale's closing remarks on his paper, as follows, should appear at the end of discussion on page 64 :

In referring to the commendatory remarks and just criticisms uttered by the gentlemen who have discussed my paper, I would say, in answer to Dr. Atkinson's allusion to the fact, that I had permitted the opinion to gain weight from my essay, that repair of tissue results by inflammatory processes, whereas he (Dr. Atkinson) maintains that it results instead by an organization into new tissue of embryonic cells, which embryonic cells are the result of retrograde metamorposis, or melting down of the original tissue.

Now, in the body of my paper, I stated that with the intricate "mass of fact and fiction which at present alone constitute our knowledge of inflammation I should not treat." However, I wish to say that I am perfectly familiar with the tenets of the school of Stricker on that subject. I know also that cells of a character similar to, if not identical with embryonic cells, are found in suppurating wounds. But I am not prepared to admit it as *proven* that repair of tissue is effected by a retrograde dissolution into embryonic cells, whence by organization as in fœtal life restoration is effected.

With respect to the use of sponge-graft, in cases such as I have narrated, I would say that I have carefully tried it, in the way, too, that Dr. Atkinson has suggested (with a cover or matrix to protect and give shape to the proliferation of repair cells), but despite every attention to minute details, both of antisepsis and manipulation, my efforts in the two cases in which I tried it soon became the seat of the most disgusting fetor, and the last state of those patients was verily worse than the first. I have seen numerous successful cases of sponge-graft in other parts of the body, but I think the mouth, with its fluid contents, temperature, uses, and environment, most unsuited for this operation, especially for slight recession or solution of gum-tissues.

In regard to my reason for abandoning the use of the dental engine in the removing and scraping away of dead bone, I would simply say in answer to Dr. Brophy that I think in removing honeycombed bone I can trace my way better by the sense of touch, and am less liable to jump and mangle my work ; although in certain cases (especially the excising of jagged or dead roots of teeth), I use the engine still. Dr. Brophy and myself agree so well I know upon our theory and treatment of maxillary necrosis, and caries, that a slight difference in the instruments we select for effecting our purpose will, I imagine, matter little as to results.

In concluding my remarks I crave permission, although possibly not strictly in order, to a device which in the retention of very loose teeth in the removal and treatment of necrosed or carious bone around their roots, I have found very serviceable. The device referred to is a part of the admirable and original application of mechanical principles for the regulation of teeth. It is essentially the method indicated by him as his method for the *retention* of teeth *after* they have been regulated by bands with tubes cemented to the teeth and connected to each other by a wire. I can not, unfortunately, take the time now, nor do I think that if I had the time, could I satisfactorily describe it. I greatly regret that Dr. Angle is not down here as was expected, in which case he could demonstrate the device in question. I have represented it by the chart which I show, and it was also illustrated in the *Medical Record* of October 6, 1888; it being in that article recommended as a splint for the treatment of fractured maxillæ, for which purpose Dr. Angle commends it. I thank you, gentlemen, for your patient attention at so late an hour.

Dr. Case's clinic should have been printed on page 121.

At the Clinic of the Twenty-Fifth Anniversary of the Chicago Dental Society, Dr. Calvin S. Case, of Jackson, Michigan, demonstrated his method of making artificial vela for congenital cleft palate. The case operated upon was a man æt. about 30, with a cleft extending through the soft and the posterior two-thirds of the hard palate.

In taking the impression, which seemed to be not more difficult than taking an ordinary impression for a partial denture—he endeavored to enforce the fact that absolute perfection was material only along the border of the cleft in the hard palate, and over that portion of surface in the roof of the mouth that is to be covered by the lateral wings of the anterior portion of the artificial palate. From this he made a mold in plaster and formed the model of the palate in modeling composition, producing the form of the "veil" by repeatedly trying in the mouth. Then by the aid of a specially-formed flask he surrounded it with parts in plaster which were subsequently duplicated in Babbit-metal. The latter were not more difficult to make than an ordinary die and counter for a metal plate.

In polishing the casts preparatory to vulcanizing the artificial palate, he showed how the first palate may be produced with a thin and abridged veil so as to be less irritating to the naturally sensitive tissues, and how subsequent ones could be easily thickened and extended, as the case required, and also in case the palate is found to be imperfect in its proportions, how it can be readily corrected by scraping or renewing the casts.

After the palate was vulcanized he took the impression for the sustaining plate, leaving this to be finished at the college.

During the clinic the doctor presented two patients—residents of this city, both wearing artificial vela made by him; and all who saw these cases pronounced them perfect in every particular. One had been worn about six months, and showed a marked improvement in vocal articulation; the other was finished the day before the clinic, having been made at the Chicago College of Dental Surgery, for the benefit of the students.

While at the college, he took impressions of two other cases—one of which he got ready for the final casts in Babbit-metal—leaving both to be completed by the students.

www.ingramcontent.com/pod-product-compliance
Lightning Source LLC
Chambersburg PA
CBHW030905050726
47500CB00009B/1091